_Z_ Cobb

Time to accept he'd sound like a fool.

Swallowing in a last-ditch effort to regulate his tone, Zach admitted, "Sam called you Cadie. I wanted to be different."

A squeak pitched from her throat. "Well, mission accomplished."

"I didn't mean it in a way that mattered," he lied.

"I better check on Ben." She shot to her feet and grabbed the baby monitor from its perch on top of a novel near the blanket, then hurried toward the house, too fast for him to try to catch her.

"Cadence!" he called.

His last-ditch effort worked, and she halted, turned back halfway to regard him warily. She closed her eyes for a second, and when she opened them again—damn, was that a trace of tears? Her knuckles tensed around the baby monitor. "It mattered to me." And she disappeared into the house.

It had mattered to him, too. But as much as he knew he was special to her, that could never match the craving he had to matter the most.

To completely belong to each other.

* * *

SUTTER CREEK, MONTANA:
Passion and happily-ever-afters in Big Sky Country

Dear Reader,

Welcome back to Sutter Creek! Readers of book one of the series, *From Exes to Expecting*, might remember Lauren catching a whiff of interest between Zach and Cadie. Well, her radar was accurate! The ski-patrol director has it bad for the single mom. And his on-the-job injury gives Cadie, a physical therapist, the perfect opportunity to solve one of *his* problems for once.

Touching his ex-Olympian body, though? Too tempting. Still healing from her rocky marriage, widowed Cadie is determined not to fall in love again—not even with the sexy, loyal man who's been her rock since her husband's death in an avalanche a year and a half ago.

Zach, who survived the fatal slide, is bound by the promises he made to his dying friend. But following through on his vow to take care of Cadie and her son makes it harder to preserve Sam's memory, and Zach has to reconcile honoring his friend and his desire to love Cadie and be a father to Ben.

I would love to hear if Cadie and Zach's journey through grief into love resonates with you. Find me on Facebook, Twitter and at www.laurelgreer.com.

Happy reading!

Laurel

A Father for
Her Child

———

Laurel Greer

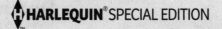
HARLEQUIN® SPECIAL EDITION

Recycling programs
for this product may
not exist in your area.

ISBN-13: 978-1-335-57398-8

A Father for Her Child

Copyright © 2019 by Lindsay Macgowan

Printed in U.S.A.

Raised in a small town on Vancouver Island, **Laurel Greer** grew up skiing and boating by day and reading romances under the covers by flashlight at night. Ever committed to the proper placement of the Canadian *eh*, she loves to write books with snapping sexual tension and second chances. She lives outside Vancouver with her law-talking husband and two daughters. At least half her diet is made up of tea. Find her at www.laurelgreer.com.

Books by Laurel Greer

Harlequin Special Edition

Sutter Creek, Montana

From Exes to Expecting
A Father for Her Child

For my parents, who modeled a love of reading
and let me consume books by the light
in the crack of the door—thank you.

Prologue

Zach Cardenas wrenched his key in the lock on the first-aid shack near Sutter Mountain's summit and drew another line in his mental tally.

One workday closer to Whistler.

Not to forgiving himself, or Sam.

But he clung to the hope that making another figurative payment on the debt he owed would ease the guilt and grief wedged in his heart.

Or visiting the accident site will be one more reminder of how watching over Cadie means keeping one promise but breaking another.

Jamming his keys in the pocket of his ski patrol jacket, he erased the unwelcome thought. In a week he'd climb on a plane. He wasn't one for countdowns, but honoring Sam's final requests had become all-encompassing and couldn't be realized until he and their buddies went on a memorial backcountry trip to British Columbia.

The ones who'd survived, anyway.

Lucky, the news had called them last spring. Zach scoffed. The reporters wouldn't have chosen that description had they been the ones left desperately digging through snow for survivors, only to board the homebound plane with three fewer passengers.

Nor would they have framed him as a hero had they known about the argument he'd had with Sam the night prior to the avalanche.

Shaking off the memory before it picked off the half-healed scab on his soul, Zach turned his attention to his friend and supervisor, Andrew Dawson.

"Day's done, Dawson. Hammond's Chute beckons." He motioned toward their skis, which were secured to one of the few metal storage racks that remained after the end-of-season cleanup. Fixing his helmet under his chin, Zach zipped up his ski patrol windbreaker, jammed on his gloves and waited.

Andrew jerked his head in agreement. He waved for Zach to lead the way to their equipment. "Let's head out."

If there was one thing that helped Zach forget, it was cutting into spring snow with freshly sharpened and waxed skis. The afternoon couldn't have been more perfect. Swathes of white sliced into thickets of evergreens that arrowed down to the village of Sutter Creek, Montana. The sun still shone but it had dipped behind the mountain, leaving a welcome chill. He started toward the narrow entrance of Hammond's Chute. Pausing briefly to gauge a good line, he took a breath and pushed himself over the lip. The regular pattern of the moguls took him back a decade to when he'd competed for the Canadian Olympic freestyle ski team in his early twenties. The rush of perfect vertical spiked his adrenaline. But the challenge was good—he needed to be in top form for when he headed home to heli-ski one of the remote ranges near Whistler.

He eyed a ridge on the edge of the run that looked decent enough to launch off. Following up a stretch of moguls with a good flip was an ingrained habit. The faint swoosh of Andrew behind him anchored him as he took the jump.

Weightless, like his stomach was free from gravity. *Bend knees... Annnnd down—*

An eerie snap, the unmistakable crack of failing plastic and fiberglass, filled his ears.

He pitched to the left. The world tilted. *No, no, no.* He focused on the mogul ahead as he tried to balance on his lone unbroken ski. He hit the center of the mound of snow and launched.

Uncontrolled. Too fast.

The green of the trees blurred with white and blue as he vaulted sideways and somersaulted. Sickening vertigo twisted his insides, singed his throat. He'd spent half his skiing career upside down. This was not that.

He hit the snow like a bent, human slingshot. Fire ripped from his knee to hip and tore a scream from his throat. He flipped forward and yelled again as he began to slide down the hill. The cold burn of snow scraping against his face kept him from completely blacking out from the inferno engulfing his left side.

Get on your back.

Roll.

Floundering, fighting the knives slicing into his body, he obeyed his instinct and flailed onto his back. Head pointed downhill, he squeezed his eyes shut against the bluebird sky. *Holy mother.* The mounds of snow jerked his body. His leg seared as if he were bouncing down a coal bed instead of a steeply pitched hill.

"Zach! Hang on!" Andrew's shout broke through the buzzing in his ears.

Trying to stop himself, Zach banged his right arm on something hard and the inferno spread to his biceps. He struggled to get air into his lungs. He had to stop. Had to be okay. His parents and sisters would kill him if he was seriously injured. And Cadie… Her sweet face filled his mind and he forced his limbs to relax as he rocketed down the slope. He wouldn't get hurt as badly if he could just stay loose. But the jolts to his body, rattling his joints and lashing fire along his leg and arm, made it damned hard not to go rigid.

Was this what his friend felt when the avalanche swallowed him?

With pain closing in on all sides, Zach refused to give in to the encroaching black.

I can't leave Cadie alone. Sam already did that.

Chapter One

"Who stuck you with construction detail? You'll be lucky if you're done by opening day."

Kneeling next to eight zillion pieces that theoretically made up a free-weight rack, Cadence Grigg ignored her sister Lauren's abrupt announcement. She glared at the sheet of illustrated instructions next to her on the floor. Driving rock music, chosen by the receptionist who'd arrived a little while ago and was happily setting up the front desk, pumped from the built-in speakers and muffled Cadie's curses.

Easy assembly. As if.

Lauren shifted on her feet and cleared her throat. With her blonde hair plaited into two sweaty French braids and body clad in workout clothes, she must have just finished up at the membership-only gym that adjoined the physical therapy facility of Sutter Creek's new wellness center. "Bit of a mess in here."

"Thanks, tips."

"I'm just saying…"

You're just saying you think I'm taking too much on.

Nerves danced in Cadie's chest. Irritation, too. Maybe once this place was up and running, her family would finally stop thinking of her as the grieving, pregnant woman she'd been when her husband died eighteen months ago. They would see her as the competent single mom and professional she was. But getting upset wouldn't help her cause. She inhaled, taking a hit of latex-and-rubber construction smells. New paint, new floors, new possibilities. For her family's venture, and for Cadie.

"It's progressing nicely," she said.

"Uh…" Lauren's gaze flitted from the stacks of boxes of exercise and therapy equipment to the half-assembled massage table crowded against a mirrored wall. "I'm sure you have a vision."

"I meant the *rack* is progressing nicely," Cadie ground out. She waved a hand at the chaos that she'd somehow turn into a functioning PT clinic before Evolve Wellness opened in ten days. "But I'll deal with all this, too."

"You sure?"

"Yes, I'm sure." She jabbed a finger at the opaque glass wall that separated the exercise space from the reception area. "Treadmills are going there. Pulley systems and exercise benches adjacent. And all those boxes are going to fill the treatment rooms. You should see the stuff I've ordered, Laur. My old boss wouldn't even know what it is, it's so up-to-date."

"Sounds great," Lauren said warily.

"No, it sounds like you're accusing me of overextending." She took a centering breath and started screwing one of the rack's support pieces onto what looked like part of a shelf.

Lauren knelt on the opposite side of the pile of metal pieces. "It is a lot…"

"And I've got it under control." She'd finish setting everything up, even if she had to bring her eleven-month-old son Ben's playpen and put him to bed here for the next ten days.

"It's not *that* you can do it, it's when. I don't want you to burn out before Evolve even opens."

"I'm not delicate, Lauren." Her jaw tensed, making her molars creak. "Ben's in daycare three days this week. And my staff is pitching in."

"But—"

"Evolve was *my idea*." She'd been working out of borrowed space since Sam's death, and she was more than ready to be in charge. She'd proposed the facility—a place where physical therapists worked alongside practitioners of massage, reflexology, Reiki and other holistic methods—to her dad as a new branch of their family's company. Wellness complemented AlpinePeaks's high-end ski-resort business model, but nonetheless, her dad had put a lot of faith in her plan. "And I will make it succeed. Starting with finishing this stupid rack."

She lined up another shelf piece on the support bar. The holes weren't flush. Grrr.

"It's backward," Lauren murmured.

Cadie's neck burned. "I knew that."

So much for being competent. She could name the six-hundred-plus muscles in the human body, but stick her with furniture assembly and she became illiterate.

Flipping the piece around, she jammed a screw through the now-aligned holes. "I can do this myself."

"Yeah, right. I'm never going to forget that IKEA shelf that you managed to turn into a wooden spider." Lauren held out her hand. "Let me look at the instructions."

"Worry about your own office. And stop being a mother hen."

Wincing, her sister retracted her hand. "Crap. Sorry. I wasn't going to do that anymore."

"I know. You're trying. Sometimes." Cadie sighed. "Were you sneaking in a gym visit before the grand opening?"

"Yeah, couldn't resist all the shiny new toys. And it was now or wait for tomorrow. There are only about two hours a day where I don't feel like puking up my morning handful of soda crackers."

"Can't say I miss that part of pregnancy."

"Can't say I've figured out any part of pregnancy that's worth it. Other than the endgame, I'm assuming."

"It is. So are the looks I keep seeing Tavish give you. It's like it's Christmas morning every moment of his day." Cadie would have given a lot to see that same look on Sam's face when she was pregnant with Ben. All she'd gotten was fear and resentment.

She tried to keep a smile on her face but it wobbled. *I'm happy for my sister. I'm happy for my sister.*

She'd repeat it until the envy receded. Because even if she'd wanted to risk falling in love again, she didn't have the time. Ben kept her running for half her hours and the wellness center was turning that jog up to a sprint. Those two things would keep her perfectly fulfilled, damn it.

Lauren plopped down on the ground. "Zach showed up just as I was leaving. Said he was doing rehab."

Cadie narrowed her eyes. Contemplating Zach Cardenas and his physical therapy—the PT he refused to let her be involved with—never failed to make her blood pressure rise. Sam's best friend could definitely add *Cadie's main source of insanity* to his excessively long list of accomplishments. *Cadence's*, rather. For some reason, he always called her by her full name. Claimed to like it. And Lord, so did she. Her spine shivered every time the smoothly spoken syllables rolled off his tongue.

Argh! In a desperate attempt to derail her train of thought, she handed her sister the Allen key. "Here, you do the screws. I'll hold the pieces together."

Lauren peered at Cadie, suspicion written on her features. "I thought you didn't want help."

"Changed my mind."

"Changed the subject, you mean."

Cadie shrugged.

"Cadence Grigg."

"Lauren Dawson," she mimicked. "Hey, are you going to change your name when you get remarried?"

"Probably. And you did it again."

"I asked you a question. Is that not allowed?"

"Not when you're avoiding talking about something. You were the one who complained we needed to get back to acting more like friends. So why'd you get a look when I brought up Zach?"

Cadie sighed. "He's just frustrating me. If I have to spend one more minute watching him compensate for his misaligned hips, I'm going to throw a medicine ball at his head." She'd spent the last three months doing her best not to look at her husband's best friend's beautiful body as he rehabilitated his broken femur and arm with a colleague at her previous workplace, but she'd had enough.

"He did look out of whack."

"He has this bee in his bonnet over finishing Sam's film this fall. They've changed the focus from an extreme skiing feature to a documentary about the avalanche. The producer's thrown in extra money to get Zach to the site where the slide occurred, given he missed the memorial trip in the spring, so he's trying to speed things along.

And he's causing more problems than he's fixing. I've been nagging him to let me help for months."

Cadie held a crosspiece against the slanted top shelf, and Lauren started screwing a nut onto one of the bolts, a look of confusion on her face. "Zach would do anything for you, though."

"Because of Sam, yeah." Sure, she'd hit the six-month mark of parenthood and woken from her sleep-deprived haze to find Zach's assets—especially his ass—irresistible. She'd slapped a "friends-only" label on the guy the minute she'd gotten together with Sam. But she was single now, and the edges on that label were peeling like the paint on her brother's ancient truck. Thankfully, Zach hadn't ever hinted at wanting to tear off the designation for good.

Lauren stilled her hand mid key-turn. "Just Sam?"

"Yes," Cadie emphasized.

Lips pressed into a wholly unconvinced line, her sister went back to her task. "Well, no matter the reason, if you can make his therapy about doing you a favor, I bet he'd go for it."

Interesting thought. And not a stretch, either. "It *is* partly about me. I want to pay him back for all he's done for Ben and me since Sam died." The guy had quit his job coaching the US Junior ski team to relocate to Sutter Creek when Cadie had moved home, for God's sake. He'd gone to every one of her maternity appointments. Held her hand through most of the delivery and kept all her loose ends tied while she was struggling with a colicky infant. Every time Cadie had needed a hand, Zach had stuck his out to help, up until the point he'd broken his arm and leg during spring cleanup. The number of times he'd apologized for not being able to pitch in over the past few months...

Yeah. That was definitely why frustration ate at her every time she was around him.

It didn't have anything to do with the way laughter made his eyes dance or how the bronze skin over his ripped muscles hadn't forgotten he'd once been a competitive athlete. So the guy was nice to look at.

More than nice.

Downright mouthwatering.

But that was all objective. She couldn't be interested in Sam's best friend. Nor could she risk the bond Zach had with Ben over a momentary physical attraction.

"I doubt he'd agree that you owe him," Lauren said. "The guy has survivor's guilt written all over him."

Letting go of the now secure shelf brace, she gnawed on one of her thumbnails. "I know. He insists *he's* indebted to *me*."

"Come at it from a professional angle, then. You need him for his reputation."

"Huh. Hadn't thought of that." Nodding, she held a support rail for Lauren. "If Zach thinks I need to be his therapist to build credentials for the new clinic, he might play along." Any publicity would be fantastic and with his gold-medal reputation—not to mention his overwhelming popularity as ski patrol director—he'd make the perfect poster boy for what her center could offer. Especially if she helped him heal faster using a combination of her PT and the other clinic services. And she could rest easier knowing she'd made a small dent in the pile of favors she needed to repay.

"How about I keep going on the rack and you go see if you can catch him before he leaves the gym?" Lauren offered.

Cadie scrunched her face—she really didn't want her sister doing work for her, especially not when Lauren had her own office to set up ahead of her official switch from doctor at the local clinic to health consultant at Evolve. But the thought of Zach spending one more minute overdoing it and causing himself further injury chafed. "You go worry about your stuff. I'll talk to Zach and then come back and finish before I need to get Ben."

Lauren shook her head but she spread her palms in surrender and stood. "I'm not trying to take over, Cadie."

"I know. But I've been working on this for a year and you've stepped in at the last minute."

"You said you were okay—"

"I am." Cadie rose and put a hand on her sister's arm. "I'm pumped to get to work with you and glad you've found something that makes you happy. But I want to be able to put my stamp on things."

A puzzled look crossed her sister's face. "But given this is an AlpinePeaks project, we're all involved in it."

Yeah, they were, and their father and brother were, too. Technically more than Cadie, because she'd liquidated a good chunk of her shares in their family's company to support Sam's dream of becoming a world-renowned, extreme-ski film star. Had he known that attempting to achieve that fame would mean dying, would he have insisted on pursuing it so hard?

A lump formed in her throat and she swallowed it. Best not to answer that question. "I know you're just trying to help, Laur. But let me take the lead. Please."

A minute later she was heading through the atrium, passing the glassed entrances of the spa and the hallway to where various energy-healing practices would take place. She hung a left past a ceiling-to-floor waterfall and entered the fitness facility. Her footsteps were the only sound in the large space—odd to have a gym without some sort of loud music. Had Zach already left?

But a quick scan revealed him sprawled on one of the exercise mats across the room, chest rising and falling rapidly. His two-day stubble failed to hide the stark defeat marking the line of his jaw. Concern shot through her. Taking stock of potential physical reasons for his unrest, she skirted around exercise equipment as she headed in his direction. Sweat dripped from his forehead into the chestnut-brown hair at his temples. A stability ball and a set of small hand weights lay within arm's reach. His crutches leaned against the pristine mirror. He'd lost some muscle mass since his accident. But not so much that he didn't have women virtually lining up outside the door to his apartment, offering to take care of him.

As if casseroles and doe-eyed sympathy would magically heal him.

No, he needed rehab. Specifically, her skill set. Which meant no more salivating over the way his thin T-shirt was currently plastered to his perfect abs. Not if she wanted him as a client.

Business, Cadie. To get what she needed—and to facilitate what Zach needed—it was time to work some emotional sleight of hand.

Breathing hard from exertion, Zach flopped his head to the side, taking in the wonder that was Cadie Dawson in yoga clothing. Tight leggings hugged those perfect legs. Her curly brown hair was straightened today, captured in a ponytail. The curve of her waist, the strength in her arms… His hands bitched loud and long over not being able to slide under her shirt, to test the softness of her pale skin.

As was becoming more frequent, something mysterious flashed in her blue eyes. He'd assumed that, after all the time they'd spent together over the past seven years, he knew all her expressions. "Cadence. Hey."

"This would be going a heck of a lot faster if you'd let me stick needles in you."

"We talked about that. Not happening."

She crossed her arms. "You must be tired. Your Canadian is showing."

He wasn't going to dignify her reference to his accent. For the love of God, British Columbians did not say "aboot." That was an east coast thing. But she liked to pretend he did to get a rise out of him.

"Back to nag me?" he asked.

"I just want you to get better."

"I thought you were pissed about my Whistler trip. About the film."

"I am. I don't think it's worth risking your rehab in order to get the film done. It can wait. Sam's not going anywhere." She let out a dry laugh, the kind that covered her increasingly hoarse tone. Well, sort of covered it. The sound came out strident.

Zach pushed himself up to sitting, leaning more heavily on his left arm. His broken right arm had complicated his recovery, delaying his ability to get up on crutches. "I have to get it done. It can't wait."

"I'm aware," she murmured.

You think you are. He'd confided in her enough for her to know how much Sam's death weighed on him. But he hadn't told her everything. Didn't want to hurt her worse that she already was.

"Your time crunch is the reason I keep nagging you about trying new techniques," she continued. "Dry needling, for one. And we could combine PT with some holistic methods from other center practitioners. You're out of alignment from overcompensating, and you need to loosen those muscles. And the program you're following isn't getting that done. Not in time for you to be tromping across a glacier by October."

He went through the painstaking motions of getting himself up off the ground. He winced as he limped the few feet to get his crutches. Why did she have to be here, seeing him hobble around? "I'm comfortable working with my therapist."

Her throat bobbed. "PT's not supposed to be comfortable."

"No kidding." At this rate he didn't think he'd be physically comfortable again for the rest of his life. His doctor had assured him he should make a full recovery, but it sure wasn't happening anytime soon. A cramp pulsed in his back and he straightened, had to breathe deeply to release the pain. He paused for a few seconds to take in another lungful of air before tucking his crutches under his arms.

"So why won't you let me help you, then?" she pressed.

Ah, one more thing he and Cadie wouldn't ever discuss. He'd literally held her upright for a good chunk of the first few months after Sam's death. He'd watched her belly grow. Had been the first one to feel Ben's kick on the outside. Had held the little guy for hours once he was born, letting Cadie get caught up on sleep after a rough labor, pretending all the while that the protective, paternal feelings clamoring in his chest were solely connected to fulfilling his promises.

Hell, Sam had begged him to watch over Cadie.

But he had to draw the line at having her massage his aching muscles. And having her as his physiotherapist would require just that. Yeah, he had no doubt Cadie would be the utmost professional during treatment. But he'd had his therapist's thumbs pressing into his ass muscles more than once. And he didn't want to know what his body would do if Cadie touched him likewise.

"We're friends. It would be weird," he hedged.

"But I've worked with friends before—" She took a deep breath. "Okay. You're resistant to letting me help you. But how about the other way around?"

"Huh?"

"If you signed on as a client and my ideas work, you could talk us up to some of your friends in the ski world. Or even just locally. Since you moved here, you've wrapped most of Sutter Creek around your pinky in less time than it used to take you to rotate through the air eight times."

"Three times," he said with a smirk.

"What?"

"I only did 1080s."

She let out a single *ha*. "Whatever. Point being, your fan club will listen to you."

Rocking forward onto his crutches, he stared at the ground. *Fan club. Not quite.* But he'd done what he could to fit in—he didn't see Cadie leaving any time soon, so neither would he.

"I'll talk Evolve up no matter what," he promised.

"I need more than that, Zach." Vulnerability cracked through her matter-of-fact expression and the breach ripped straight to his core. "I need you to be my client. And if you want to be ready to shoot that video come the fall, you need me, too."

I need you to take care of them, Zach.

The words weren't so different. Memories slammed into him, raising bumps on his skin. Echoes of biting wind and blisters stinging his palms and his exhausted arms shaking under the weight of Sam's broken body. And returning to Colorado and holding Cadie instead.

She, at least, had given him something to focus on instead of his grief.

But as always, he'd focused on her a little too much.

Zach swallowed against the fist of guilt clamped around his windpipe.

The fact he'd been falling for Cadence since the day he and Sam met her in a Steamboat Springs bar was moot. She'd only ever had eyes for Sam. That made it a hell of a lot easier for him to keep his second promise to Sam: not to let Cadie or Ben forget Sam. Which meant getting that video done and memorializing Sam on film. And since switching to Cadie's care would accomplish that... Damn it.

He'd have thrown up his hands if it weren't for his crutches. "I give in. I'll call my current therapist tomorrow, tell him I'm switching into your care to start dry needling."

Her jaw dropped for a second. Then a brilliant smile spread across her face, lightening her blue eyes so that they resembled a clear winter sky. "Seriously?"

His brisk nod failed to shake out the dread building in his stomach. "You know me, and you've watched me ski enough to know my body. This is the right change to make."

She paused for a second, seeming to puzzle how to get around his crutches, before going on her toes and flinging her arms around his neck. "We'll start right away. Meet me in the pool at one tomorrow."

He gripped the handle of his left crutch and let go of his right to give her a cursory pat on the back. Just like his sisters.

As if.

Hugging his sisters was nothing like hugging Cadie. Hugging Cadie was all about her soft breasts pressing into his chest and the smell of cherries he always caught whenever he was within a few inches of her hair. The sense that this woman's arms held the secrets to happiness.

Not for you, idiot.

Steeling his body, he took hold of his right crutch again. And, thank God, she backed away, too.

"I really think this is best for you." The brightness in her eyes faded a fraction. "But before I take you on, you need to promise me something."

He dragged a hand through his hair. What was one more promise to tangle in all those he'd made to Sam already? "What's that?"

"I'll do everything I can to get you healthy in time to go on your filming trip. But if you're not ready, you can't go."

He inhaled sharply as his gut clenched. "Deal."

She'd better get him rehabbed in time. Because no matter how ready—or not ready—he was, when the helicopter lifted off to take the filming crew into the backcountry, he'd be on it.

Chapter Two

Meet me in the pool at one tomorrow.

Cadie cringed as yesterday's instructions to Zach echoed in her head. What had she been thinking? She floated in the shallow end of the public aquatic center and watched him amble along the pool deck toward her, supported by his crutches. Shirtless. Showing off a perfect sprinkling of trimmed hair leading down abs that could grace a fitness magazine. Her skin tingled and not from the water kissing her limbs. Yeah, the pool had been a *brilliant* move. If only she could change history, go back to when she was three and not learn how to swim. Then she could throw herself in the deep end and be done with it. Drowning sounded way smarter than taking him on as a client.

Nice choice of words, Cadence.

Her mental sarcasm landed like a boulder in her stomach. For one, this was her choice, and a necessary one. She could truly help Zach and, in doing so, could boost Evolve's reputation. And she needed to start doing all that without thinking of crappy death comparisons. *Sorry, Sam.*

Lacquering on a smile, she waved at Zach, who slid into the water and crossed the pool with long, muscled strokes. He stopped a yard or so away, close enough that she had to tilt her chin a little to keep her attention on his face. He was a good six inches taller than her own five-seven. The height difference held so many possibilities. If he were healthy he'd be able to pick her up and—

She pinched her thigh under the water. *He's your client. Your best friend. Do not screw that up.* "Ready to work?"

He nodded curtly.

"We'll start with walking back and forth across the shallow end and work up to a jog." The pool wasn't too crowded—a parent-and-tot class occupied the splash pool and a dozen-odd people were swimming laps in the deep end.

"Uh, sure." Following his gaze was a challenge. It seemed to land on her tank swimsuit for a second and then everywhere but, darting from the waterslide to the diving platforms and settling somewhere on the wall behind her. "Walking. Okay."

She raised a brow. "Quite the conversationalist today."

A faint rosiness bloomed on his cheeks and he rumpled his already disheveled hair, dampening the strands with his wet hand. "I…"

Way to make your client feel self-conscious, idiot. "Zach. Deep breath. You've done this before."

"Right."

Ri-ight. She loved the way he drew out his vowels sometimes. His voice had become her touchpoint when she'd been in her darkest moments. Blaming herself and Sam and the universe.

Smiling encouragingly, she motioned for him to follow her. He complied. And as long as she kept her eyes fixed on the oversize lap clock on the wall, and her attention on counting their steps backward and forward, she could almost ignore the way the water swirled around his waist, drawing her gaze to the delicious V of muscle dipping below the ripples.

Good grief. Focus. And not on that.

She went to pinch her thigh and brought her elbow up, accidentally deflecting off his forearm.

"Ow." He brought his other hand to his arm in an exaggerated gesture.

"Oh, no. I'm so sorry!" Heat flooded her face. Could she not do anything right these days?

"Cadence." His thumb dragged along her jaw and she blinked long, trying to ignore the shimmering trail on her skin. "I wasn't serious. You barely touched me."

"I know," she said, trying to throw a *duh* tone on the retort.

He moved his hand from her face to her shoulder. His pupils flared wide despite the bright pool lights and his mouth parted. Snapping it shut, he yanked his hand away.

"What's the next exercise?" he blurted.

"L-lunges." And thankfully his legs would be under the water while he did them, because the unyielding strength of Zach Cardenas's thighs could make a nun renounce her vows. Neck heating, Cadie splashed her skin and silently begged the clock to tick faster. Why couldn't she have stayed in her blissful, mothering fog, unaware of the perfect definition of his quads?

She worked him through a set of lunges and leg balances, filling the time with chatter about Ben's attempts to climb the toddler-focused play structure Zach and her dad had built in the backyard a few weeks before Zach had taken his header down Hammond's Chute. Her son was just figuring out walking, and many a face-plant awaited Ben in his immediate future. Hopefully Zach's calming influence could moderate the daredevil tendencies her son had inherited from his father.

Before Ben's birth, she'd been clueless about how much she could love another being. It consumed her, filled in all the cracks in her soul left after the earthquake that was Sam. His life, and his death. "Get this. I left Ben in his bedroom for all of a minute yesterday to answer my dad's landline, and when I get back, he's made his way to the bathroom and is holding on to the edge of the bathtub, crowing for 'Baff!' and trying to figure out how to climb in. He's growing too fast."

She tried to laugh but her heart cramped.

Zach's lips curved in a forced smile. Good to know—she had him working to the point of not being able to comfortably talk. Either that or he didn't like Ben growing up, either. Maybe both.

He finished up his leg balances and she rushed him into the next exercise. She held out two pool noodles. "Pink or orange?"

A hint of amusement warmed his eyes to a mossy green and he grabbed the candy-pink foam tube.

"Sure, leave me with the one that clashes with my bathing suit," she teased, tucking the tube around her back and under her arms. Using the water as resistance, she took him through another thirty minutes of therapy. Hopefully he wouldn't notice the series of half-moon indents on her leg from the number of times she'd dug her nails into her skin while he'd done push-ups against the pool wall. The effort it took not to stare at his chest made her pulse race.

Yeah, right. That effect is from the chest itself, not the effort.

After finishing a set of squats that made him flinch in a way she didn't like, he glanced at the clock. "We done?"

"In the pool? Almost. Swim a few laps to cool down and then hit the showers. But I want you to meet me at Evolve. My office is still a disaster, but the table's set up. And I want to work you through some physical manipulation."

She kept a visual track on him as he pushed off from the bottom of the pool and headed for the other side, which was cordoned off as a lap lane. Did he depend on his left arm and right leg in the water as much as he did on land? She'd probably find some impressive knots of muscle in a few places. She knew how to loosen those.

The knots in her stomach were another story.

"Evolve in twenty?" she asked once they'd gotten out of the pool.

He grimaced and toweled off his hair.

His clear reticence sent the butterflies in her stomach even more atwitter than they'd been while trying not to stare at his pecs.

Client. Professionalism time. "Are you more sore than normal?"

"Nah."

Ah, so he was in a constant state of pain, then. Stubborn man.

"Hey. Have a seat." She pointed at the plastic deck chairs where they'd left their towels. He eased into one of them and she took the other. She made sure she had full eye contact with him before she continued. "We don't have to do this today if you don't want to. We don't have to do this at all. I know I can help you. And successfully rehabilitating you will benefit Evolve. But if it doesn't feel right to you for us to work together, you need to be honest about that. Our friendship is more important to me."

He held her gaze, but his eyes were more guarded than usual. He'd definitely thrown up an emotional barrier of some sort. Sucking in a breath, he shook his head. With his hair still wet from the pool, the strands stuck together. One clump fell across his forehead. He pushed it back. "I should get my hair cut."

Non sequitur much? And from her angle, the length flattered. Demanded to have fingers run through it. His nervousness, however, broadcast a clear "don't touch" message.

"Seriously," she said. "What's wrong?"

Tipping his head back, he stared at the observation deck for a few seconds before reverting his attention to her. "I'm tired today. Can you give me something to do at home instead?"

His deferral hollowed her chest until emptiness tugged at her ribs. Tired? Or reluctant? Had he picked up on her attraction? Her stomach curdled. If she lost his friendship because she couldn't get her freaking hormones under control, she'd never forgive herself. "I—I can do that to a point, but I want to work you through some range of motion exercises before I draw up a home program."

He shrugged and stood. "I'm not going to screw up my recovery with one day of solo rehab."

He'd been screwing up his recovery for months, but his mouth was too drawn to remind him of that. "You have a stability ball at home? And some two-pound weights? Draw the alphabet while holding those—I'm assuming you've done that before?" She paused until she got a brisk nod from him. "And tie a stretch band to one of the support posts on your back railing and do three sets of fifteen extensions per side." She demonstrated the fly motion she wanted him to do.

"That's wimpy stuff, Cadence."

"Yeah, well, until I have a more complete assessment of where you are, I'm not giving you more. Your swimming today demonstrated an acceptable range of motion for your right arm versus your left. But you're still walking with a heck of a limp."

He made a face.

God, how awesome would it be to kiss off that— *That nothing. Nothing, nothing, nothing.* "And meet me here tomorrow at 9:00 a.m. In the afternoon, we'll meet at the Evolve gym. Plan for a month of two-session days. As long as you're serious that you don't have a problem working with me."

"This is fine. We'll be fine. I'm excited to work with you." Jamming his crutches under his arms and slinging his towel over his shoulders, he smiled at her.

The false tilt to his lips made the emptiness spread from her chest to her stomach. She watched him as he disappeared into the locker room, wishing to the bottom of her heart that he was telling the truth. And knowing he wasn't.

His health demanded she persist, though. She couldn't watch him suffer anymore. But in helping him heal, she had to make sure she didn't irreparably harm their friendship. She wouldn't have made it through the last year and a half without him. And the year and a half to come, and the one after that… She needed him to be her rock then, too.

After showering off the chlorine, Zach made his way back to his truck and hoisted himself in. Proof of some progress, at least. A few weeks back he'd been stuck trading vehicles with Cadie because he couldn't get into his pickup. She'd done him that favor, even though she didn't owe him anything. And he'd switch to her care if it would make a difference for her career.

Gripping the wheel, he filled the cab with a string of profanity. Filthy enough that he half expected his Colombian-born, Catholic father to reach across the thirteen-hundred kilometer distance separating them to cuff the backside of the head. Didn't matter that Zach was a grown-ass man of thirty-two—his dad was the best of fathers but hadn't lost his strict standards for his children.

And it wasn't like blue language was going to extract Zach from the tangle he'd agreed to.

Backing his truck out of the parking spot, he took a centering breath. *Suck it up. No complaining.* He'd follow through with the rehab. And with keeping his feelings to himself.

As he wended his vehicle through the streets of Sutter Creek—an attractive mix of the ski-town architecture Zach had grown up with in Whistler, along with some western elements for flavor—he gripped the steering wheel and hardened his jaw. He'd promised Sam he'd watch over Cadie and the baby for as long as they needed.

And for your own sake. He winced as his conscience prodded him with the truth. Yeah, selfish motivations painted a lot of what he did for Cadence Grigg. Because even though he wasn't ever going to be able to tell her he loved her, he could sure as hell show her without words. Without hands, too. Cadie would have to touch him for rehab purposes. But he'd still keep his hands off.

If he ventured beyond their usual hugs, actually took the opportunity to savor her smooth skin under his palms… His groin tightened and he groaned. Time for a new train of thought. Maybe he could sneak into the lodge office and throw some paperwork around. His doctor had limited his hours and activities at work, but he did what he could to stay in the loop. Not nearly enough. The entire summer season would be burned by the time he was ready to return in full capacity.

A few minutes later he crutched toward his office in the bowels of the Sutter Mountain base lodge. He scowled at the smiling marmots painted on the ski-school side of the hallway. He did not need that level of saccharine cheer this afternoon. Those stupid animals could shove their joy straight up their cartoon asses. Must be nice, being a wall decoration and not having to worry about physio that wasn't progressing fast enough or promises to your dead friend.

Choking on the thought, he gulped and tried to swallow the pain. Yeah, his left leg was bugging him and his right side had seized up like an overzealous boa constrictor, but at least he was alive. He had no right to gripe, not when Sam wasn't able to gripe at all. And even if both his doctor and Cadie didn't think he'd be ready, he'd figure out a way to get up that mountain to finish Sam's project.

He shoved the office door with a little too much force. It banged into the wall with a metallic crash as the attached venetian blind reverberated with the impact.

The two occupants of the room startled.

Tavish Fitzgerald, Cadie's brother-in-law-to-be, raised his tawny head from where he sat at Zach's desk and shot Zach a questioning look.

At the closer desk, Andrew Dawson, Cadie's older brother and Zach's boss, spun in his chair. His reading glasses failed to hide the purple smudges under his eyes. His dark brown hair looked like it hadn't seen a comb in a day or two. The classic parent-of-a-newborn look. Zach had seen it on his own face a few times after helping Cadie in the months after Ben's birth.

"One of these days you're going to owe me a door, Cardenas," Andrew griped.

"I'm good for it." Zach hobbled into the room and leaned against the edge of the long wooden top of the retro entertainment center they'd converted into a food-prep station. Better than easing into a chair and showing off his lack of grace and the degree to which his leg was pissing him off. He took in Andrew's empty cup and the fresh pot brewing in the coffeemaker. "I take it the kid hasn't figured out that 'sunup' means awake and 'sundown' means asleep?"

Andrew slid his glasses off and scrubbed his face with both hands. "Nope. He likes to tell us all of his woes from about two to five in the morning."

"Brutal." Zach propped his crutches against a nearby shelf and then reached across the narrow space between the desk and the wall to grab Andrew's mug. Filling it from the carafe, he stirred in a heaping spoonful of sugar. "Here. Caffeinate."

"Thanks." Andrew grabbed the drink, took a long swig then coughed. "Right. Hot."

Tavish snorted. "Sleep deprivation have you forgetting the basics of temperature, genius?"

"In about seven months this'll be you." Andrew pointed a finger at Tavish. "Just wait." He eyed Zach. "What's got you so cheerful today?"

"I— Physio problems. Thought I'd come in to get some work done—distract myself—but I see my desk is taken." Zach tilted his chin at the mess of photographs and draft promotional materials scattered across his desk. "I'll grab my laptop and go work in the staff lounge."

"No, you'll go home and rest," Andrew instructed. "Doctor's orders. And mine."

Zach scowled at Andrew, who was well practiced at flipping between buddy mode and boss mode. "How the

hell is sitting and editing the policy-and-procedure man-
ual not resting?"

"Anyone can do office work. Only you can get you
better. And I need you sparky for opening day."

"Oh, I'll be on skis in plenty of time for a December
opening." And he'd be hiking along the avalanche site
far before that, getting Sam's film done.

"That's not what my sister said," Andrew threw back.

"Which one—the nosy one or the nosier one?"

Tavish snorted.

Andrew glared at his brother-in-law. "You wouldn't
be laughing if Lauren were here."

"I'll make it up to her."

"Yeah, didn't need to know that. But I meant Nosy
Two, not Nosy One."

"Cadence won't be able to tell you my secrets anymore," Zach grumbled. "Client confidentiality and all
that."

"Client?" Andrew asked.

Zach nodded.

"About time," Andrew crowed. "Don't know why it
took you so long."

And Andrew never would. What guy wanted to know
that his sister was starring in a friend's nightly fantasies?
Not that Andrew had a leg to stand on there—he'd married Tavish's sister, Mackenzie—but still. Time for the
easy answer, even if it would make Zach sprout feathers
and start clucking around the office. "She had to talk me
into it. Needles aren't my thing."

"But skiing is," Andrew said.

Zach lifted a shoulder.

Tavish ran a hand through his dark blond hair. "Lauren texted me. Told me I was supposed to help convince

you for the sake of the new wellness center. Apparently they want you as a poster boy?"

"So goes the story." Zach slumped and then straightened as he caught himself cradling his right elbow. Damn it. He really needed to stop favoring his injuries. His arm didn't really hurt anymore. But his back sure did, from having thrown himself out of alignment by not taking it easy.

"I don't buy it," Andrew announced.

"Why?"

"As if the center's going to be anything but successful. They already have a full slate of reputable wellness providers, and the promotions team has sold a ton of gym memberships and spa packages." Andrew narrowed his eyes. "This is about Cadie somehow."

Slapping the desk, Tavish got a "Eureka!" look on his face. "When she and Lauren weren't talking to each other last month, it was all about Cadie's independence. This is probably that, too."

"You taking up psychology instead of photography, Fitzgerald?" Zach grabbed a mug and busied himself making his own beverage. He managed to do it while putting minimal weight on his left leg, avoiding the inevitable winces and tugs that came along with standing on his injured limb. Best not show Andrew how much Zach still needed his crutches.

"Um, if anyone's going to know Dawson women, it's Andrew and me."

Zach kept silent. Yeah, Andrew and Tavish knew the Dawson women well. But so did Zach. And Cadie had been increasingly awkward with him since his accident. So if joining her client list could facilitate them getting back their once-easy equilibrium? Another reason to go along with her request. Even if it meant having to take cold showers every night.

"This project is Cadie's baby," Andrew pointed out. "She knows it's going to succeed because the company name's on it and people trust AlpinePeaks's ventures. But she wants to be the one to make that happen. With the way she's poured herself into it, I'm thinking she's using it to prove herself."

Tavish waved a hand at Andrew. "What he said."

Zach's heart panged and he needed to sit down. Not because of his aching thigh, for once. "That's part of it."

"What's the other part?" Tavish asked.

"She thinks she owes me," Zach said quietly.

Andrew's dark brows rose. "So let her pay you back."

"She doesn't need to."

"And when are you going to feel like you don't need to owe her anymore?"

Zach blinked at Andrew's pointed question. Was he that obvious? He didn't make a habit of talking about the promises he'd made to Sam, but then, Andrew wasn't stupid. "I don't."

"Why else would you move here, man?" Tavish asked.

Okay, so Tavish wasn't stupid, either.

"I will cop to keeping an eye out for her. She was wrecked and pregnant and it seemed the prudent thing to do."

"Big sacrifice," Tavish mused.

He didn't know the photographer as well as he knew Andrew—Tavish had been out of town up until recently—and the blasé observation made Zach blink.

"Sam was my best friend," Zach explained.

Andrew's eyes narrowed. "And Cadie is…"

"My best friend's *wife*." *Oops.* Zach hadn't meant for that to come out so harshly. Time to backpedal, and quickly. Before either of his friends figured out how often he had dishonored Sam, picturing Cadie as *his* wife. Ben as *his* son.

And he didn't have the will to force the fantasy back into the mental vault he'd built the moment he'd spotted Sam flirting with Cadie at that bar in Steamboat Springs.

He and Sam had both honed in on Cadie, who had been dancing with a friend that night, dark hair streaming around her bared shoulders—she'd been wearing a sleeveless top that was probably illegal a hundred years ago. An ill-timed visit to the john had meant Sam moved in on her before Zach had the chance. There hadn't been a thing he could do about it then, and that was twofold now. He wasn't going to throw another shovel of dirt on his dead friend's grave by pursuing Sam's widow.

"Pretty sure there's a statute of limitations—"

Zach cut Tavish's lighthearted statement off with a glare.

"—or not," the guy finished.

"Yeah, not." Andrew shot Tavish a disbelieving look.

Zach cringed. He'd come to the office to think about something other than Cadie, not to spill his guts to her brother and her sister's fiancé. Unplugging his laptop and tucking it under his arm, he leaned on one of his crutches and moved toward the door in an awkward, hitching hobble. "Coffee klatch is over. I'm going to get some work done."

But something told him that Cadie was going to be drifting throughout his brain, no matter what he attempted as a distraction.

Chapter Three

Zach would give Cadie one thing: she took pain from "hurts so bad" right through "hurts so good" and straight back into "hurts so bad." And pain and Zach were on a first-name basis. Even without his experience on the Canadian Olympic team, his year as Sutter Mountain's ski-patrol director and skiing and boarding in Sam's extreme backcountry films had brought him his fair share of aches and injuries. But the rehab Cadie had put him through for the last five days ranked only below the surgery required to fix his femur. She hadn't even given him the weekend off. Her devotion to working every centimeter of his body gave the impression his recovery was the difference between life and death.

At least the intensity stopped him from thinking about her sweet ass.

Sometimes.

He lay like a piece of overboiled spaghetti on a mat in the wellness center's membership-only gym, pretty sure his perspiration-soaked shirt and hair made it look like he'd taken a dunk in one of the hydrotherapy tanks.

Fifteen weeks and a day after his accident, and what he used to take for granted now drenched him with sweat. He'd been out of his wheelchair for a while, but was still struggling with the impacts of having been sedentary for so long. He could barely handle half-hour spurts on the elliptical trainer without collapsing.

Cadie crouched at his splayed feet, still wearing the smirk she'd sported while beating up on him during both their sessions today. "Had enough, superstar?"

"Not unless I'm ready to get revenge on Hammond's Chute for putting me in this position."

"Keep working like you are, Zach, and you will be," Cadie said, encouragement spread across her face for the first time since he'd hobbled in this morning.

Goddamn. Too much kindness from Cadie and his mind would start wandering down dangerous trails. Enticing trails. Trails marked with clear out-of-bounds signs.

Shaking his head, he planted his soles on the floor, knees bent, and reached out his hands for support as he stood. Cadie gave him just enough of a pull to help him to his feet without completely demolishing his pride. "I like you better when you're mean, Cadence."

Her eyes widened for a second before she snapped her eyebrows into an irritated scrunch. "Fine, then. Get your butt on the recumbent bike and loosen up those muscles you just abused. Then we'll cool you down."

Ha. Not likely. He'd felt hot and itchy since they'd started pool therapy last Friday. Cadie in a bathing suit continued to blow his mind. Four effing languages at his disposal but his ability to string a sentence together ran for the hills the minute he got a glimpse of her in a modest one-piece. Today's outfit, a stretchy workout top and skintight exercise pants, wasn't much better. He envisioned each piece of clothing laid end-to-end, paving his path to purgatory for lusting after his best friend's widow.

"I'm going to go grab a few things from the PT office." She pressed buttons on the recumbent bike's display to set the speed and resistance and then turned to leave. He forced himself to stare at the ticking numbers instead of appreciating her tight rear as she disappeared through the gym's entryway.

Working with her was not easy. But as he spun on the bike, he had to give her credit. He was going to be sore as anything tomorrow, but a good sore. The things she'd had him do had loosened him up for sure.

She came back a few seconds before the timer on the bike beeped for him to stop, a stapled booklet in her hand. He wiped the sweat off his forehead with the bottom of his T-shirt, obscuring his view of her chewing on her lip. The sound of fluttering paper caught his attention and he let go of his shirt hem.

Kneeling on the ground, she was fumbling for the papers she must have dropped.

"Everything okay there?"

"There are boxes stacked from here to heaven in the reception area," she said, the words rushing together like the waters of the Gallatin River after a good rain.

"Your shipment arrived?"

"Finally. I'm so relieved—having the private workout area in the PT clinic is a key part of our philosophy." She pressed her palms to her cheeks.

He smiled at her flustered state. No small thing, starting a clinic from the ground up. Maybe she needed a break. "What are you and Ben up to for dinner tonight?"

Her eyes widened a little and she darted her gaze to the side. "Uh, I'm going to go get him from day care once we're done here. I'm cooking for my dad tonight."

Normally she'd invite him over, so her hedging didn't sit well, like an air bubble in his stomach that needed to pop.

"Anything you want me to do before our next session?" he prompted, grabbing his crutches off the floor and swinging his healthy leg over the bike to stand.

Throat bobbing, she nodded. "We worked a lot on loosening up your hip. You need to ice tonight. And I want you to use your foam roller in the morning. Here. Instructions." She thrust the thin sheaf at him.

Tilting one side of his mouth up, he motioned to his crutches and his inability to carry anything.

She reddened. "Oh, crap, of course. Sorry. I'll put it in your backpack."

"Cadence, I was giving you a hard time," he said to her retreating form as she hurried over to the pack he'd left leaning against the front counter. "I could have stuck them in my pocket."

"I don't mind." She jammed the sheets in the top compartment of his pack and straightened.

"Hey." He swung over to her and laid a hand on her shoulder. "What's up?"

"I don't have time to deal with the shipment today, but if I leave it, tomorrow will be even worse."

He *wished* he were that busy. At least he'd seen some progress with his physio, but otherwise, he was at the toddler-having-a-tantrum stage of boredom. "Put me to work, then."

Cadie's mouth stretched, that *ehhh, no* look. "You've had some productive sessions, Zach, but not enough to haul weight machines around."

He sighed. "One of these days you really need to lie to me."

"I—" Her gaze shifted to the floor.

Was she keeping the truth from him? His stomach twisted. "If there's something I should know, just tell me. Don't sugarcoat my recovery."

"I'm not." She coughed. "Promise."

Fine, but she was holding something back. He hated the dishonesty. He swung his backpack onto his shoulders. "Tell you what. You stay here, get a few hours in. I'll take your car and get Ben, and I'll help your dad with dinner. I'll even put Ben to bed if you like. We can switch vehicles after you're done."

Sadness flashed in her eyes. "I'm not going to ask you to put Ben to bed for me. What kind of mom—"

"The kind who has an open house in three days," he said gently. "Parents have to work sometimes. And you're doing the work of two. I love spending time with Ben. You know that."

Longing pulled at his chest. He wished he could support her in every way. *Let it go. You aren't Ben's dad. You can't be.*

Chewing on her lip for a minute, she leaned back against the reception desk and toyed with the end of her ponytail. "You always know what to say."

Patently untrue. He'd said a whole lot to Sam the night before the avalanche, and putting his friend in that scattered, distracted frame of mind had been deadly.

"I'll take you up on the offer for day-care pickup, though," she continued.

"Good."

"Just be careful getting him in and out of the car."

"No kidding."

"What? I don't want you to screw up your progress by hauling my son around."

"I won't. Lifting twenty pounds between a stroller

and a car won't hurt me. And I'll push the stroller one-handed so I can use one of my crutches."

She sighed. "Fine. But I want to try some visualization techniques with you before you leave. It's not my specialty, but I know enough."

He let out a dry laugh. "There's a condition on letting me do you a favor?"

"Yes. I'd rather you be resting. But if you're insisting, well, visualization it is."

Zach managed to keep his grimace off his face. He'd been visualizing all day. Mainly images of her face, her flat stomach and her long legs. Not necessarily in that order. But his libido needed to give his brain a break and start changing those mental pictures to ones of himself trekking down a steep BC mountain slope. Otherwise he'd end up failing Sam again. Twice over.

"I don't see why you needed to tag along," Cadie grumbled at her sister as she pulled into their dad's driveway around 7:00 that night.

"I don't see why you're being so weird about me coming," Lauren retorted, sliding out of the car. "Tavish is out tonight, and no way am I passing up Zach's schnitzel."

Cadie had to give her sister that. Zach's mom's recipe was killer. She slammed the door of his truck, entered the house and passed straight through the high-ceilinged living room into the kitchen at the back of the home. Lauren followed.

Their dad stood at the kitchen island, chopping cabbage. "Get all your work done, Cadie?"

She dropped her utilitarian mom-purse on one of the stools tucked under the island and shook her head. "I need it perfect for the open house. Are you going to be at home tonight? Mind if I head back after dinner?"

"You say that as if I've been allowed to have a social life since my heart attack," he said lightly.

Lauren squeaked in protest.

Cadie shot their dad a dirty look. "You *should* have a social life."

"Hypocrite," Lauren muttered.

Cadie jabbed her sister with an elbow. "I need to say goodnight to my baby before he falls asleep. Is he with Zach? Where are they?"

They. It fit, the unity. The only person more bonded to Ben than Zach was Cadie herself.

"Upstairs."

The second floor of the house was quiet, so she tiptoed down the hall in case Ben was already sleeping.

She peeked into his room. The lamp on the changing table cast gentle light across the pair dozing in the padded rocking chair.

Her heart melted.

Zach's hands cradled Ben's back. The baby must have been fussing at some point, because Zach's hair looked like he'd just run through a windstorm.

Lines of exhaustion marked his eyes but his mouth was relaxed. And Ben lay on Zach's mouthwatering chest like he hadn't a care in the world.

Smart baby, picking that particular spot to nap.

And stupid me, for wishing I could take Ben's place.

Shaking her head at herself, she snuck into the room and arranged Ben's sleep sack in the crib. Her baby was going to complain when she moved him. He was completely at peace in the arms of the man who'd never once hesitated to step up. Had never stated he didn't think he could be a parent.

Zach is not Ben's father.

How many times was she going to need to remind herself of that? Probably until she stopped wishing it was the truth and stopped comparing Zach and Sam.

Because Sam came up short, every time.

Guilt pressed her insides. For thinking such terrible thoughts about her husband, and for letting Zach save her ass, over and over.

He made too many sacrifices for her. Tonight, even. He should be at home resting after a hard day of therapy, not pitching in with Ben. Pragmatically, she knew that as a single parent she was only hurting herself if she didn't lean on the people who loved her. But she'd leaned so much in the year and a half since Sam died that she'd developed a permanent tilt.

Zach let out a sleepy snort, and she glanced at him. He had the thickest eyelashes, and—crap, it was totally crossing a line to sneak peeks of him while he slept.

She ripped her gaze away from his beautiful face, knelt on the rug and started cleaning up blocks and cars and stuffies as quietly as possible. But her gaze kept drifting back to the rocking chair. Last summer she'd made a study of watching him. Sitting at his desk with his hands tunneled into his hair. Taking kids tandem across the Wild Life Adventures zip line course. And more recently, dripping with sweat as he worked his tail off in rehab. The slow shift from objective appreciation to actually wanting to jump his bones risked toppling the scaffold she'd erected around her life.

It's just physical. I can control that.

Her stomach growled, as if mocking her confidence as well as reminding her she'd skipped lunch and had only managed to finish half her toast this morning because Ben had refused to eat anything except the food off her plate.

"Yikes, I'd better make double the schnitzel." The

low rumble of Zach's voice hooked deep in her core and she bit her lip.

He smiled drowsily, another hook anchoring into her soul. Yeah, she was never getting those out.

"Enjoy your nap?" She peeled a protesting Ben off Zach, gave him a snuggle and settled him in the crib. The minute she handed him his blanket bunny, his eyes shuttered closed.

"Needed the Zs." Zach limped over and rubbed her back. He peered into the crib, expression tender. "You make good babies, Cadence."

Her pulse skipped. "Thanks. And thanks for helping. You're…"

God, how to finish that?

He let her off the hook, suggesting they go downstairs and finish making dinner.

Lauren, who was tossing a salad, eyed Cadie suspiciously as she reentered the kitchen with a crutching Zach on her heels.

"I need your expertise, Cardenas," Lauren announced.

"With dinner?" he said on a yawn.

"No, with checking out places on the mountain that would work for a wedding ceremony."

"I can think of a few. Want me to go up with you, point them out?"

Lauren pointed at him. "Done. Tavish and I have some time tomorrow afternoon, if that works."

"For sure," Zach agreed.

Cadie blinked, first at her sister and then at the man who for some reason thought he should be tromping around on the mountain with his crutches.

"Tomorrow?" she bit out.

"The forecast is awesome," Lauren said. "And I'm all set for Saturday—"

"Must be nice." Cadie winced at the admission implicit in her sarcasm.

"Do you need—" Lauren snapped her lips shut, obviously having remembered their conversation from last week.

"—a hand?" Zach finished. "What still needs to be done?"

What didn't need to be done was the more pertinent question. "With my equipment arriving so late, I have another treatment room to set up, as well as one of the weight machines. And then it'll be party stuff to take care of. We have some subtle decorations, and I need to do a final check with the caterer and the DJ and all that. Essentially everything you're going to be freaking out about come New Year's Eve." Tavish and Lauren had decided they wanted to get married before the baby was born, but were giving themselves as much time as they could to plan. Lauren would be seven months along at the wedding.

Zach whistled. "Big list."

"Yes. And you shouldn't be going up the hill, either." She sent him a "We'll talk later, mister" look, which he returned with a bemused blink.

Lauren snapped her fingers. "Tell you what, Cadie. You come help us tomorrow—be a fourth set of eyes up the mountain. We need opinions. Then we'll come back and help you. It's a *trade-off*."

Cadie sent her sister a pained expression. The offer was worded in a way that she'd be foolish to say no. She couldn't argue with a trade. Nor could she let her pride get in the way of rocking the open house arrangements.

And Lauren knew it.

"Fine. But prepare to work like dogs tomorrow."

* * *

"If you think you're attacking the equipment setup with Tavish when we're done here, you're sadly misinformed," Cadie grumbled at Zach in a low enough voice that the hum of the lift cable likely prevented Tavish and Lauren from hearing her.

They were occupying the left side of a quad express chairlift that connected the base of Sutter Mountain with the mid-mountain Creekview Lodge. She'd ridden many a chair with Zach—they'd skied together a ton before and after she'd married Sam. God, she'd spent her last year of her bachelor's degree and her whole master's degree schlepping between Denver and Steamboat Springs. But it had been a while since she'd shared a lift with Zach. She'd stayed off the mountain last winter. And she couldn't remember ever sitting next to him on a lift without eight layers of clothing between them.

Today they both wore shorts. And hers had ridden up. The only barrier between her skin and his was the layer of thin technical material covering his muscular thigh. His hand was resting on the bar and that was only a few inches away from her leg, which was *bare* and would have served as a *better* resting place. And if that hand happened to slide up, to caress—

She pressed her hand to her heating cheeks and bit down on the inside of her lip.

"Cadence?" His eyes narrowed.

"Huh?" Damn, he'd said something and she'd missed it. Would he guess where her mind had gone? Would he...? Ah, crap, he was talking again. *Pay attention.*

"—didn't give me grief for wanting to come up the mountain."

Phew. She could guess what she'd missed. His surprise, likely. "Yeah, well, I thought about it. I don't want to risk your leg buckling when you get off the lift."

He snorted. "Me, neither. Good thing it slows to turtle speed when the chair detaches. I'll be fine."

"Yeah, you will. Because you're going to let Tavish carry your crutches and will let me help you off."

"Seriously, Cadence?"

"Seriously, Zacharias?"

He grumbled but twisted his face in capitulation.

He seemed happy, though. More relaxed, at least physically. Every once in a while she still caught a stiffness to his smile that had her wondering, but he'd lost last week's nervousness. And the muscles in his left shoulder and right hip no longer felt like granite. Well, they did, but not in a knotted way. Just your garden-variety, ridiculously-built-athlete kind of way.

She'd savored every minute of getting to manipulate them.

A minute later they were approaching the top of the lift. She eyed Zach until he handed his crutches off to Tavish with a sigh and lifted the bar. "Okay. You win. How do you want to play this?"

"I want you to step off with both feet and quickly step forward with your good foot. Hold on to my arm while you do it."

They managed the maneuver without too much difficulty.

Well, his steps weren't too difficult, anyway. Only marked by a small hitch.

Her heartbeat, on the other hand, sounded like an out-of-step high school marching band. His grip tightened on her forearm as they moved to the side, out of the way of the chairs rotating on the overhead track.

"How's your balance?" she asked, throat tight.

"Good."

If she didn't know better, she'd have thought there was something in the air, because his tone sounded as raspy as hers. And his hand shook a bit as he took it off her arm.

Tavish passed over Zach's crutches. Zach secured the supports under his arms.

How was it even fair, him showing off his biceps like that? Mouth dry, she cleared her throat again.

As Zach gave them directions to the nearby lookout and set out along with Tavish at his side, Cadie hung back with Lauren.

"Cough drop?" her sister offered.

"Why?"

"You've got a frog in your throat."

Cadie's pulse skipped. Last week she'd managed to convince Lauren that she wasn't attracted to Zach. She needed to keep up that ruse. "Must be the altitude."

"Oh, is that what we're calling it these days? Altitude?"

"Lauren…"

Her sister jammed her hands in the pockets of her lightweight, purple hoodie and tilted her chin in Zach's direction. "You sure you want to work with him, hon?"

Want? Oh, yeah. She wanted. A week of touching him therapeutically had only ramped up her desire to touch him *non*-therapeutically. But she couldn't have a fling with her best friend. He deserved more than superficial, and she couldn't do deep. She'd had a relationship fall apart once, couldn't handle the thought of the same happening with Zach. "Working together will benefit both of us."

"Is it? I'm getting the feeling—"

"He's my client. And Sam's best friend. So wrong on all counts."

"Not sure he feels the same."

Ahead, she saw Zach's broad shoulders flinch. He must have hit a rock with his crutches or something. The guys were at least fifty feet ahead, so no way could Lauren's voice have carried. Could it? She shushed her sister just in case.

"Oh, as if he heard."

Cadie elbowed Lauren. "He could have."

"Watch." A sly smile crossed her sister's face as she called out, "I could so go for sex against that tree right now."

Neither of the guys reacted.

"See?" Lauren said smugly.

Cadie let out the breath she'd been half holding. Okay. So Zach hadn't heard Lauren's speculation. Good. But Lauren's studious expression, now locked on Cadie's face? Not so good.

Nor was the pulse between Cadie's thighs at the suggestion of sex against a tree.

"So—" she cleared her throat to lower her too-high pitch "—how did the meeting with the caterer go?"

Talk of canapés and a macaron tower and an early fall weekend road trip to Seattle for dresses filled the rest of the walk, saving Cadie from having to admit her worries about the upcoming months of therapy with Zach. After a couple more minutes they caught up to the guys, who stood with their arms braced against a wooden railing that edged a wide platform overlooking Moosehorn Lake.

"Zach, this is where Mackenzie and Andrew had their wedding pictures done," Cadie pointed out.

"Yeah, you don't like it?"

"It's fine, but why did you need to play tour guide? You could have been home icing."

Zach twisted his head to glare at her, an uncharacteristic warning. Fine. She'd give him heck later, when they didn't have an audience.

Lauren waved a hand at the men and the vista beyond the lookout. "That is one fine view."

Cadie nodded. "It'll be just as stunning with snow…"

"Mmm, and Tavish will be in a tux, too. Delicious."

Tavish turned, gaze smoky, and barked out a laugh. "Come here, Pixie. Tell me your thoughts."

Lauren wedged herself in between Tavish and the railing, and the two bent heads and started hashing something out.

A pang struck Cadie's chest. She crossed her arms and walked over to the corner of the lookout. Leaning her rib cage into the wooden barricade, she swallowed. When had Sam last looked at her with the passion her brother-in-law-to-be regarded her sister? A year before he died? Two? Hard to avoid how their relationship had been faltering far before their unsolvable quarrel over whether or not to become parents. It hurt to recognize the faulty cliché of her actions, that she'd married him, hoping it would improve their problems.

A hand landed on either side of her elbows, hemming her in. She glanced over her shoulder. Zach had discarded his crutches a few feet away and stood with his weight on his good leg.

"I'm not responsible for that look on your face, am I?" he said, voice serious.

She stared out at the expanse of summer-blue sky and pines, his nearness prickling along every inch of her back. "You will be if you keep shifting your weight to your right."

The boards creaked behind her. "Taskmaster."

"That's what you hired me for." She gripped the railing with both hands. It would be so easy to lean back, to have him sandwich her close like Tavish did with Lauren. So easy, and so wrong. She leaned forward instead. "You shouldn't have come here today, Zach. The ground is so uneven—"

"I walked all the way out here for Andrew and Mackenzie's wedding pictures last month. You didn't nag me then."

"You still had your brace on at that point—you were more stable. And I nagged the heck out of you."

He chuckled. "Well, the next time I come here will be in the winter on skis. You'll have to be okay with it by then."

His cavalier tone grated on her sense of professionalism. She whirled around.

Son of a mother. The foot and a half of space between them felt like a mere inch, with his stubbled face angled toward her. *Psst, Cadie's fingers. Touch me,* that jawline begged.

She focused on making eye contact. Not that that was much easier given the sun was glinting in his eyes, replicating the sparkle of summer light on Moosehorn Lake's green surface. "Skiing this winter isn't a guarantee, Zach."

His arms fell from the railing and he rocked back. "What's the point of me working with you if I'm not going to be ready to ski?"

"I want to get you ready to ski. We'll do every possible thing we can to make that happen. But it's not a one-hundred-percent situation."

"Changing your story some now that you've got me on your client list, Cadence."

"No, I haven't. You're twisting what I said."

"How?" he snapped.

Blood thrummed in her ears. Zach never argued with her. This wasn't how their relationship was supposed to work. "I made you promise you wouldn't go on the memorial trip if you weren't fully healed. Wouldn't that imply that I didn't promise you would be skiing come winter?"

"No, it meant I might not be skiing come *October*, not winter." Pain, but not the kind rooted in physical suffering, flashed across his face. "And given there's no way I'm missing the filming trip, I'll definitely be ready for the season start-up."

Definitely was a dangerous word when it came to rehab. She sucked her lower lip under her top teeth, unsure of how to be both truthful and encouraging.

He studied her face and sighed. "Work smarter, not harder."

"Exactly. Focus."

Focusing sounded perfect. None of this stupid attraction. No giving in to the pull of desire. And for the immediate future, she might have to pull away from him a little outside of work. Whatever it took to get him healthy and protect their friendship in the long-term.

Chapter Four

By one on Saturday, Zach was stifling yawns. The four-hour-long open house was almost a wrap. He'd been busy, but man it felt good to have a task to accomplish—the measly ten hours a week the doctor had limited him to at work were not cutting it.

Today, Cadie had put him to work in Evolve's hexagonal, glass-roofed foyer, chatting up potential clients. He'd heard nothing but praise for the building, especially for the use of materials reclaimed from an old barn on Cadie's aunt's ranch. The programming seemed popular, too. A couple hundred Sutter Creek residents had come through the center, putting a good dent in that day's catering and lining up to purchase gym memberships and health and wellness packages.

He'd just finished explaining the rehab program Cadie had developed for him to one of his buddies from the county's search and rescue team when a gentle hand landed on his elbow.

A hot bolt of want speared through him. Elbows were the new erogenous zone, apparently.

"Time to take a break, Zach," Cadie admonished.

"Looks like I should say the same to you," he murmured, brushing a handful of flyaway strands of her dark hair behind her ear. Purple smudges marked the skin under her eyes. "You going to take a day off now that this is over?"

Uncertainty tugged at her mouth.

"Cadence," he said, "you need sleep and sunshine." Two things he was limited in helping her get. Sleeping—obviously out. And his busted leg made outdoor adventures tricky. "Why don't we borrow Andrew's boat tomorrow? Take Ben for a spin on the lake? Or an easy canoe? My arm's feeling up to it."

"You'd probably be fine." Her cheek shifted as she chewed on the inside of it. "So yeah, you should get out for some light activity tomorrow. But I have stuff to do with my dad. Sorry. Maybe another time."

Disappointment stung his insides, a bigger pinch than he should be feeling after finding out a friend had a perfectly understandable reason for not being able to make plans. Trouble was, putting distance between them meant he didn't get to see Ben as often, and that plain sucked. He loved the kid as much as he loved—

Enough of that, Cardenas.

"Well, my schedule's wide open." He forced out a light, joking tone.

"No, it's not. Your ass is going to be in my office at 9:00 a.m. every day this week, and in the pool come the afternoon. You're going to eat, breathe and sleep rehab for the next month. I want you off those crutches soon."

"I know. I want that, too. And yeah, I'm seeing you twice a day for physio, but I still want to hang out now and again."

"Let's—" her throat bobbed "—focus more on your

therapy for now. I'm going to be better able to meet your needs if I'm thinking of you as a client rather than a friend."

His brows knitted. While he wanted her attention on getting him back on skis ASAP, he didn't see why she couldn't compartmentalize—friend stuff off the job, work-only in the clinic. She was the one who'd promised she would be able to do just that.

Unless… Was she struggling with her feelings? Could she be starting to think of him…?

Nah. She'd never indicated she thought of him in any way other than platonic. Her nerves during their therapy sessions had to be from her being more invested in his recovery than she would be with another client. Or—*damn.* Had she picked up on *his* feelings? Noticed when the affection, the yearning, had broken through his wall? He'd carefully crafted that emotional barricade. Fear struck him every time he noticed a crack, or felt a chunk crash to the ground. The appearance of those breaches had been happening with alarming regularity. And if she'd figured him out…

"Did I do something…?" No, better not to go down that road. He squeezed the grips of his crutches. *Dumbass.* Years of keeping his feelings close to the vest wrecked by less than two weeks of her talented hands manipulating his broken body. He'd have been tempted to cancel their deal, go back to his old therapist. But Cadie was doing a better job—he'd made a ton of progress just this week. And his conversations with potential Evolve clients today made him think her theory about his opinion holding clout with the outdoor sports community in the area held merit.

"Did you do something…?" she echoed, prompting him with a hand.

"Never mind." The words soured on his tongue. He tilted his chin at the short line of people waiting to speak to the main receptionist. "Go talk up your clients. I'll do the same."

She shook her head. "You've been on your feet enough. Head home."

"But we're not done—"

"Head home," she repeated. "Getting healthy means trusting me to know what you can handle."

He sighed. Couldn't argue with that. Saluting her, he swung toward the front door. Maybe it was fortunate she didn't want to head to the lake tomorrow. He needed the time to patch up his inner wall, make sure she never caught a hint of his interest again. She wanted to think of him as a client? Well, he could be the best damn client she'd ever had.

The Friday after the open house, Cadie finished up with her morning appointments and ran out to her car to retrieve a box of advertising materials she'd picked up on her way to work. Their opening days had buzzed with activity. She should go out tonight, celebrate. Maybe Zach would—

No. Bad idea. She could celebrate with her dad and Ben. Starting the minute she dropped off the bulky flyers, in fact. She wasn't on the afternoon schedule, her first time off in weeks. She tried to scurry back from her car unnoticed. Someone would invariably nab her and slow her up, so she pulled out a rude but necessary trick.

Pinching her phone between her ear and shoulder, she pretended to be deep in conversation as she approached the entrance. She hip checked the accessible door button. Impatience flooded her system. Could the freaking thing open any slower?

She rushed through at first moment and something caught her toe. The box and her phone went flying. Her sharp hands-and-knees landing jolted her body. The heels of her hands stung, abraded by the laminate. She sucked in a long breath.

"Cadie?"

"Cadence!"

Two familiar voices blended together. Zach's gruff concern a low note in opposition to higher-pitched surprise from her friend Garnet James.

Cheeks burning, Cadie knelt and brushed off her smarting palms. She groaned at the flurry of advertisements littering the floor.

Garnet rushed over and started to reload the box. The willowy redhead did a little bit of a lot of things around town. She'd recently quit her part-time job at the coffee shop on Main Street to allow herself time to build her fledgling holistic practice at Evolve. She also volunteered for search and rescue and worked for the ski patrol. They'd been friends in high school and had become even closer since Cadie had returned home.

Concern crossed Garnet's freckled face. "You okay, sweetie?"

"Yeah, fine." Cadie joined in the cleanup effort, glaring at Zach when he grabbed his crutches in both hands and moved to squat.

"You've done enough today," she instructed. They'd had nine appointments this week. He'd been a model client. Dedicated and distant. Exactly what she'd asked for.

But the opposite of what she *really* wanted.

His face hardened. "Easy, General."

Oh, those were fighting words, especially when the tired lines around his eyes were deeper than they'd been a few hours ago. "I thought I told you to go take a nap."

"Garnet squeezed me in for an acupressure treatment," he grumbled, using his crutches as support while awkwardly bending and picking up a handful of spilled flyers. "And we always have lunch on Fridays, so I thought I'd come get you. We can walk to the diner."

"Not this week," Cadie blurted.

His brows drew together. "No?"

She shook her head. Going out for lunch was the exact kind of friendly activity she wanted to restrict while they were working together. But she couldn't explain that, not in front of an audience.

Their audience of one eyed them suspiciously.

Zach must have clued into Garnet's curiosity because he didn't protest.

"I have to pick Ben up early," Cadie explained further. A half truth.

He stared at her, a silent reminder that there was nothing stopping them from picking Ben up together. A few weeks ago, that would have been the norm.

He tossed a last stack of flyers in the box. "I'll head home then."

Nodding curtly, she swallowed. "See you Monday."

He stalked away—well, hitched, really, but the stiffness in his shoulders suggested he'd be stalking out were he not on crutches.

Cadie winced. Her stomach felt as heavy as the wood-and-slate mosaic she, Andrew and Tavish had struggled to hang on the feature wall of the atrium a few weeks ago. She ached to call Zach back, crawl in his arms and never let go.

Garnet sat cross-legged on the floor, straightening the promotional materials into tidy stacks inside the box. "Zach's not the only person who needs a nap. For someone who's gone all-in on a facility that promotes balance, you've got some stellar bags under your eyes."

Cadie narrowed said eyes. "Thanks for the reminder. Ben's decided to regress with his sleep training because of course he'd wake up three times a night for all of opening week."

Garnet paused, a thick clump of paper clutched in both hands. "Aw, he's protesting the extra day-care days?"

"Seems to be." She sat down on the other side of the box from her friend. "And it's not going to get better—I'll essentially be working full-time from now on."

Guilt crawled in her chest. A few nights of hearing her son call out for her at three in the morning twisted the knife of not being able to do two parents' worth of work. Marriage hadn't been all roses. But she still wished Sam was here to see Ben toddling in the backyard or awkwardly pitching his favorite foam ball across the family room. Or to take on some of the parenting load.

Ben would never want for a male role model—Zach was as devoted to her baby as a man could be—but Sam never getting to meet his son was an irreparable wound.

If he'd wanted to be a parent. I'm probably better off...

Her throat burned. She hated when her brain went rogue, throwing out reprehensible suggestions. Her counselor had told her that it was normal to have a range of emotions while grieving, but Cadie hadn't been honest with the woman, not fully. She refused to believe it was okay to feel relief, no matter how badly she and Sam had argued prior to him leaving for Whistler.

Yeah, he'd made it very clear that he, unlike Cadie, wasn't sure he'd wanted to be a parent. They hadn't spoken again. Had he had a change of heart while on his trip? While dying on a search-and-rescue helicopter? She hadn't worked up the courage to ask what Zach knew.

The mystery ate at her but she suspected the real answer would be worse. And given Zach had assured her
Sam's last words had been about loving her, she'd taken
the cold comfort.

She'd never had to question if Zach wanted a relationship with Ben. He held her son through giggles and wails
and croup coughs.

He'd held *her* countless times, whenever she needed it.

Wow, she missed him holding her. More than she
missed being held by the husband she was supposed to
be grieving, and what did that say about her? The question chewed a hole in her gut.

"Cadie?" Garnet said, clearly not her first attempt to
get Cadie's attention.

"Yeah, sorry?"

"Have you tried the lavender insert in the teddy bear I
bought for Ben? If you heat it up, it might help him with
staying asleep."

Cadie shook her head. "He refuses to sleep with anything except Bun-Bun." Ben insisted on having his fuzzy
blanket bunny, lovingly made by Cadie's aunt, with him
at all times. "But I could try putting the sachet inside
his pillowcase. It has a zipper, so he wouldn't be able to
get at it. Worth a try. And maybe I'll pull out the Sleep
Sheep, try some white noise."

Garnet's face turned serious. "You know this is normal, right? Regression? It happens all the time—sleep,
toilet training, if there's a stage, kids'll find a way to
screw with you."

"I—" Cadie scrubbed her eyes with her fingertips.
"I just want to make sure I'm doing a good job. With
Ben… And here…"

"Why would you think you weren't?"

She shrugged. "It's only been a week. Bit early to

judge Evolve's success. And as for parenting, doesn't everyone think they're going to permanently mess up their kid?"

"Fair point."

"Why'd you lie to Zach about lunch?"

Garnet's tone was so gentle that Cadie almost missed the challenge in the words. She froze. "Huh?"

"You're super easy to read, sweetie."

Cadie stiffened. "Lunch wasn't going to work today."

Her friend smiled but a load of rebuke was packaged in the friendly curve of her lips. "But not because of Ben."

"I don't have to go for lunch with Zach every Friday. We're not freaking married." Her cheeks immediately heated again at the thought.

Garnet blinked. "Uh, I know. But Cadie…"

Nerves skittered along her spine at Garnet's curious tone. "What?"

"Have you and Zach ever—?" Her friend's cheeks turned scarlet.

Matching heat rushed into Cadie's face. "No."

"But you wanted to?"

"No." Cadie shook her head and strands of her ponytail stuck to her suddenly sweaty neck. "I mean, he's nice to look at and all, but that wouldn't work."

Reaching out and rubbing Cadie's arm in understanding, Garnet sighed. "The energy sparks off you, though."

"Not all energy is positive, Garnet."

Tugging her lip between her teeth, Garnet stood. "It's good to be attracted to someone. You're allowed, you know, Cades. To move on."

Cadie bristled and followed her friend to her feet, heaving the filled box off the floor. "I know that." "Allowed" didn't play into it. She knew full well it was okay to find love again after loss. She just didn't get why anyone would be crazy enough to want to make themselves that vulnerable again.

"Okay, so do something about it."

"I'm not going to pursue Zach, for heaven's sake."

"That's fine—I get you have too much history there—but there's nothing saying you couldn't go on a date with someone else."

"Maybe at some point. We'll see." Because even if she decided to go off her rocker and open herself up again, the only person who came to mind was Zach.

And screw that. No way would she lose another man she loved.

I don't love him. Not that way.

After dropping the box at the front desk and a couple more minutes of small talk, she made plans to meet up with Garnet for coffee on Sunday and then fled the building. She needed a distraction from Zach Cardenas and all his golden glory. She had to get him back into the platonic box she'd kept him in since they'd first met. Her stupid needy body, the one that hadn't been touched in any way that mattered for over a year and a half, was fighting to recategorize Zach. She needed to up her resistance. But for now she craved an hour where he didn't surface in her mind every two seconds.

After leaving Evolve, she picked Ben up from day care and headed home to play with her son and get some dirt-under-the-nails therapy. After lunch and Ben's nap, she set him on a blanket under a shady willow and alternated between pulling weeds and helping her son stack cups.

A half hour later her dad ambled out of the house and eased down on the grass next to Ben. He'd either changed or hadn't gone in to work today, because he wore a frayed gray T-shirt and a pair of striped board shorts. His ease of motion warmed her soul. He was making good progress from his recent heart surgery. She still intended to keep a close eye on him, though. Make sure he didn't overdo it. The afternoon sun caught the silver in his short, dark hair as he blew a raspberry on Ben's chubby baby arm. "Wondered if I'd see you today or if you'd be holed up at work again."

"Says the guy who barely sleeps in the weeks following a grand opening," she said.

"You're sure you don't want my help?"

"How many hours a week are the doctors letting you work?"

He made a face. "Twenty."

"Something tells me you have more than enough to fill those hours without helping me out." He'd seemed happy with how his management team had been stepping in since his heart attack, but Cadie knew it chafed that he wasn't able to fill his usual CEO duties.

"It hasn't all been wins lately," he said. "Still haven't been able to convince Jenny to sell me her pie recipe. Best she'll offer is for us to buy them wholesale and heat them up on-site."

Jenny Wong owned the Australian pie restaurant around the corner from Evolve and baked a pepper-steak number that pulled in tourists from dawn until dark. Her dad had hoped to add the pastries to the menus at the base and mid-mountain quick-service restaurants.

"I'm sorry, Dad. I know you don't like losing a business deal."

"It's okay. More important to have good relationships with my fellow business owners."

Cadie smiled. That was his usual way. Everyone loved Edward Dawson. In return, he loved them back, especially his kids. And Cadie wanted to make sure she deserved that love. Living up to her older brother and sister sometimes took more effort than she'd like. Par for the youngest-child course, right?

Right.

And now she was answering her own questions. Awesome.

He cleared his throat. "How'd the week go with Zach?"

Gah, so much for having an hour to clear her mind of Zach's green eyes. She didn't look up from the weeds she was pulling. "I can't talk about a client, Dad. You'd have to ask him."

"I didn't mean specifics. But he seemed frustrated when I ran into him in the lodge the other day." He started stacking Ben's cups into a tower and laughed when Ben knocked it over after he got it four cups high. "Uh-oh!" he said in a singsong tone and he stuck his hands under Ben's armpits.

"No lifting," she barked.

He froze. "Right, boss."

"Sorry. I didn't mean to snap."

"It's okay." He narrowed his blue eyes. "But why so touchy?"

Cadie plunked the spade down, stripped off her gardening gloves and turned, cross-legged, to face her dad. The cool grass on the backs of her legs contrasted with the still-hot-in-the-shade afternoon air. She blew out her frustration in a single expulsion. "I need to start being more independent, I think."

"Because of me?"

"No…" Though they probably should have a conversation at some point about her living at home. Moving out might be a good step to proving she was taking steps toward being whole again.

"Because of your sister?"

She shook her head. "By my choices."

"Which choices?"

None she was about to share with her dad. But she had to give him something or else he'd get suspicious. "After Mom died, was there a point when you realized you needed to move on, or did it happen slowly?"

Her dad opened his mouth but didn't say anything. Focusing on Ben, he offered the baby two fingers. Her son stood and bounced on his little legs, showing off his six pearly little teeth in a smile. So much like Sam, that mouth. Same wheat-blond hair, too.

So long as Ben didn't inherit his father's unreliability, he'd do okay for himself.

Sam was not unreliable. I had unreasonable expectations.

Shoving down the truth that loved to pop up when she was least prepared to deal with it, she plastered on a happy expression. Sitting with her dad and Ben in the sunshine? Who was she to ask for more?

"Pa-pa!" Ben crowed, and her dad broke into a grin. "I seriously cannot get enough of that."

"It's pretty great."

Her dad's smile faltered. "But as for your question, I guess it happened slowly. Though there were a few moments when your aunt Georgie gave me a figurative kick in the pants not to lose myself to AlpinePeaks and miss out on your and your siblings' teen years."

Chest tightening, she asked, "Do you think I'm doing that with Ben?"

"No." A thoughtful look crossed her dad's face. He stretched out his legs so that he could give her son a horse ride on his knees. "But it's something to be aware of."

"Yeah."

"I think you're doing well, Cadie. You'll know when

it's time to move on. I assume you're talking about dating?"

Heat rushed into her face. "Not exactly."

"No?"

His suspicion didn't surprise her. She'd avoided talking about Sam since the funeral. How could she be honest about her feelings when so many of them were ugly? Her family had nagged her to open up for the first month or so after Sam's death, until she'd lost it on them, insisted she was going to counseling, and that if she wanted to spill her guts, she'd initiate. They had respected her request since—for the most part.

He stroked Ben's wispy hair with a hand and pierced her with a knowing stare. "There's no time frame, Cadie. You'll just slowly find that it feels a little better every day. And one day the better feeling will outweigh the grief. You'll never not miss Sam. But it'll get to the point where you'll be able to accept that he'd want you to find someone new to love."

Ah, the classic assumption that she missed Sam like crazy. Sure, there were times his absence clobbered her until she had to sit down. But there were also moments of the opposite. Moments that reminded her that love wasn't worth it, couldn't be relied on. "We'll see."

"Sometimes I wonder if Zach's interested in you. There have been a few times over the past while, especially at Andrew and Mackenzie's wedding, where I thought I saw sparks between you two. Lauren did, too."

Panic ran up her spine. "Uh, no. The only sparks between us are because I've been nagging him to let me be his therapist. And now that's solved. Back to same old, same old."

Mouth set in an unconvinced line, he stared at her

for a few seconds before focusing on Ben and making trail-riding noises as he bounced the baby on his knees.

Yikes. That was one too many people asking her about Zach. The last thing she wanted was for her dad or siblings—or for the rest of Sutter Creek—to think she and Zach had something going on. With him as her client, she had to make sure people only saw a professional relationship. What was the best way to get that across? Deflection, probably.

"Why haven't you dated, Dad?"

"I have."

She shook her head and pushed her hair behind her ear. "I know you see women. I mean dating, as in being part of a couple."

"I've never been able to be on a date without comparing her to your mother. And that's not fair. So I haven't let things get serious. I'm not writing it off. I'm looking for the person that will allow me to not compare. When I feel like I'm no longer looking for Jane's replacement."

Cadie hadn't been on a date since Sam died. But she knew that if she ever did go, she sure as anything wouldn't be comparing him to Sam. *No, my measuring stick would have green eyes and the best laugh and a smile as wide as the Montana prairie...*

She must have had an odd expression on her face because her dad smiled encouragingly. "You'll find your feet again."

"Eventually."

Lying to her father was the worst. But she wasn't about to share the degree to which her relationship with Sam had faltered. That was better left in the past.

Chapter Five

Zach snuck into the lodge safety office mid-afternoon the next day. Anything to keep his mind off how he'd usually be hanging out with Cadie and Ben. Distracting himself at work took subterfuge, though. Andrew had made it exceedingly clear that Zach was not to show his face at Wild Life Adventures, the outdoor-activities business that kept Sutter Mountain afloat during the summer, beyond his doctor-approved shifts. But his gut told him he was close to getting full clearance, so taking part of his day to tidy up a little around the office wouldn't hurt anyone. Andrew, out on a rafting day-trip, wouldn't know who to blame for the organization. And when Zach did come back full-time, he'd rather it be to an office that didn't look like it had suffered a nuclear strike.

Two hours later he had the paper mountain on his and Andrew's desks sorted into the correct trays and filing cabinets. Previously scattered and heaped equipment lay in bins marked to go to the biking, climbing and rafting outposts. And his back and hip barked at him that he should have taken a break after thirty minutes.

Steps sounded in the hall and he stumbled to sit in his chair before he got caught kneeling on the floor with his hands in the accounts receivables file.

A redhead peeked through the doorway. "Andrew, we're all cleaned up at the climbing—oh! Zach! Good to see you." Garnet James grinned at him. "Didn't know you were back at work."

"Only for two half shifts a week. I, uh, forgot something I needed to take to Edward, so I came in to grab it." He swiveled back and forth a little using the toe of his hiking sandal and tried to look innocent.

Garnet scanned the room, gaze landing on the tidy piles of paper and now-cleared floor. "And whatever you'd forgotten was buried under the mess that was here this morning that some well-meaning but likely now-sore-as-hell cleaning fairy dealt with?"

He shrugged, wincing as his shoulder pinched.

"Cadie'll be pissed if you overdo it."

"Well aware."

She snapped her fingers. "Wait, are you stopping by Edward and Cadie's today?"

"Maybe?" He'd committed to the cover story. Better run with it. "I have some paperwork from my doctor that needs his signature, but it can probably wait."

"Oh. I have a, um, a jacket in my car for Cadie. If you *were* going by there, you could take it with you..."

He suppressed his protest that Garnet could hold off until Monday to return the jacket. Guess he'd have to swing by Cadie's place. Would she be annoyed, given her request they not hang out on weekends? Irritation pricked the back of his neck over having to worry about this—even before Sam's death, he'd dropped by Cadie and Sam's place whenever he'd felt like it. And damn it, he needed baby snuggles. "Yeah, sure."

Stuffing a few random sheets in a folder to make it look like he was actually taking something to Edward, he stuck the papers in his backpack. He followed Garnet out to the parking lot.

"You look stiff," she admonished as she retrieved the garment from her trunk and passed it to him. "Good thing I'll see you for more acupressure on Tuesday."

"Yeah, I'll be there after physio." He'd try anything that gave him the slightest result until he was back to 100 percent.

Waving at Garnet, he climbed into his truck. Ten minutes later he pulled into the circular driveway in front of the massive, chalet-style home where the Dawson kids had grown up. Cadie claimed not to mind living with her dad since she'd moved from the apartment she'd shared with Sam in Steamboat Springs. She'd told Zach the house was big enough that having a parental roommate didn't cramp her style.

Probably would if she started dating again, though.

Cadie, dating.

Her hand, tucked into the grip of some other guy. Her lips— Zach's stomach turned and he forced the thought out. Snatching the jacket off the front seat, he crutch-stalked to the front door. He rang the bell and waited. No one answered. Cadie's car sat in front of the closed garage door, but maybe she was out for a walk with Ben or had gone off with her dad. He could leave the jacket on the door handle…

The door swung open and his breath caught. The combination of her dark hair piled on her head and her cheeks fresh-air flushed always punched the air from his lungs. But throw in the yoga bra and sport skirt covering—or rather, not covering—her body and he had to hold back from airing out his T-shirt, which was now sticking to his back. He'd have blamed the afternoon sun, but only Cadie could crank his temperature that much.

"I didn't mean to, uh, pull you from your Saturday." He held out the jacket. "I ran into Garnet at the office and she asked if I could bring this by."

Confusion darkened her blue eyes as she studied the cloudless sky. "Because I needed a coat during a heat—" Her expression flattened. "Were you always planning to come by?"

"She thought I was bringing something by for your dad."

"Thought?"

"Long story."

Planting a hand on a hip, she glared at him. "You already worked Tuesday and Thursday this week."

"Yes…"

"So why were you at the office?"

Because I needed something to do to keep me from thinking about you. She still hadn't taken the article of clothing and he felt like an idiot standing there with his hand out. He tucked the jacket in the crook of her cocked arm and awkwardly turned to leave. "Errand done. I'll get out of your hair."

"Wait. Why are you so stiff?"

He froze with his back to her and glanced over his shoulder. "Because I broke my femur?"

"Ha, ha." She stomped down the three front steps to face him, eyeing him owlishly. "What were you doing at work today?"

"Just organizing a few things for your brother."

Her face softened. "Always cleaning up after people. Come in." She skirted around him, motioning for him to follow her into the house.

"Thought we weren't socializing on weekends," he

said, unable to keep the bitter statement inside. He hated that he'd given her reason to put distance between them.

"We're not," she said evenly, taking him through the front living room and the kitchen and out the back door into the spacious yard. "I have about forty-five minutes until Ben wakes from his nap. I'm going to make you walk around the yard a bunch of times and then stretch."

"Yes, ma'am."

Like he had for all ten-and-a-half hours of appointment time this week, he kept his expression neutral and his eyes forward while she directed him in circles on the lawn like an army general. Though an army general had never dressed like that. The handful of teal, crisscrossed straps snugged between her shoulder blades drew his gaze despite his best efforts. Closing his eyes, he leaned further into a seated hamstring stretch and growled at his muscles' continued resistance. Had it not been for that goddamn faulty ski, he'd be directing rafting tours and climbing sessions and bike trips and keeping himself sufficiently occupied so that the beachy smell of Cadie's sunscreen would have been miles from his consciousness. His sanity.

"Further, Zach," she urged.

He complied, leaning forward. She centered a palm at his lower back and the other on his shoulder and adjusted the angle of his spine. Heat enveloped his torso and his crotch. Ah, hell. The thin material of his shorts would do nothing to conceal that.

"Cadence? Won't Ben be waking up soon? I should head out, let you get on with your afternoon," he said, hoping she attributed the tightness in his voice to physical effort rather than the straining front of his shorts.

"Not yet. Lie on your front on the blanket."

Well, that took care of one of his problems. He settled

on the quilt with his face to the side and his arms resting in a loose circle over his head. He waited for her to explain what new and torturous paces she intended to put him through, but all she did was press a thumb into a persistent knot at the base of the left side of his neck.

He hissed out a breath and clutched two handfuls of blanket.

"That okay?"

"Define 'okay.'"

"Do I have your permission to massage your shoulder?"

"Yeah, sure."

"Relax your hands. I'm going to try to get this knot to release."

He released his grip on the patchwork fabric. There was something about the pain that went along with therapeutic massage that intrigued Zach. It was almost addictive, knowing the sharp jabs and slow aches would eventually let go and relief would flood in.

They didn't talk, but the yard wasn't silent. The crack of club on ball from the neighboring golf course competed with bees humming in a nearby lavender patch.

She worked at the muscle and the surrounding area with a combination of stroking thumbs and insistent fingers. After a few minutes she hit a particularly tender point.

He grunted, gritting his teeth.

"Sorry. It's tenacious. I'll needle it on Monday." Her tone made it sound like her jaw was as clenched as the muscle in his back. "Can you lace your fingers together and rest your forehead on them? I'd like to try working on your neck with it straight."

Following directions, he tried to make a pocket with his fingers so that his breath didn't give his face too much of a steam bath. The quilt smelled like it had been washed in lemon laundry detergent and hung out on the line to dry. Cadie's sheets probably smelled the same—

And there went his groin again, getting all excited about something he'd never discover the answer to. He racked his brain for something to take his mind off her sheets and her fingers. Conjugating German verbs, calculating mountain slope angles—none of his standbys worked.

With smooth, sensual strokes, she worked the tension from his neck, lulling him and lighting him up simultaneously. Not exactly a clinical massage anymore. He melted into the ground. The blood thrummed in his veins.

"Tell me—" *your fantasies* "—about this quilt," he croaked.

"Uh, my great-grandma made it." Two of her fingertips slid into the hair at his nape, drawing little circles at the edge of his skull.

He shifted against the blanket. "Holy mother. Why haven't you been doing that all week?"

"What, mentioning Gee Gee?" she teased.

He snorted. "Obviously."

"I'll make a note in your client file to do that more often." Sliding all her fingers into his hair, she traced lines and whorls on his scalp. His mind blanked beyond the tiny fireworks sparking under her fingertips.

"Relax," she said. "Your hands are tense again."

"Right." He exhaled and fought to unball his fists. "Fair warning—I'm a sucker for a head rub. If you keep at it, I might take up residence on your lawn, Cadie."

Her fingers froze. "Oh. Well." She withdrew her hands and his scalp rioted against the lack of attention. "I should—" the blanket moved against his hip as she scrambled back a few feet "—I mean, that's probably good for today."

His gut bottomed.

Way to freak her out, Cardenas. Rising on his elbows, he turned his head to survey the damage. Her wide eyes looked extra blue against her pale skin. A hint of white teeth peeked out from under her upper lip—her jaw wasn't dropped, but it definitely didn't suggest ease on her part.

"I'm sorry. I was joking, obviously. I'm still going to respect you wanting to keep things professional—"

"You called me Cadie." She hugged her knees to her chest.

"I did?" Uh-oh. He never used her nickname. That extra layer of formality had always served its purpose well. "Does it matter? Everyone calls you that."

"Not you."

The seriousness of the gaffe had thoroughly dealt with the situation in his shorts. He rolled to sitting. "No." He shook his head slowly. "Not me."

"Why is that?"

His heart rate picked up.

What had he told her in the past? She'd asked before and he'd said… What had he said? "I like how it sounds?"

"No, that's what *I* told *you* about you calling me Cadence. You just told me you liked it. And that's crap, Zach. What's the real reason?" Her gaze, slightly wild and a whole lot of vulnerable, sucked him in. A desperate, animalistic need rose in his belly, clawing for him to gather her up and soothe away her upset.

His mouth was too dry for him to sound unaffected. He worked his tongue along the inside ridges of his teeth, trying to get some saliva going. Nope. Not happening. Time to accept he'd sound like a fool. Swallowing in a last-ditch effort to regulate his tone, he admitted, "Sam called you Cadie. I wanted to be different."

A squeak pitched from her throat. "Well, mission accomplished."

"I didn't mean it in a way that mattered," he lied.

"I better check on Ben." She shot to her feet and grabbed the baby monitor from its perch on top of a novel near the blanket, then hurried toward the house, too fast for him to try to catch her.

"Cadence!" he called.

His last-ditch effort worked and she halted, turned back halfway to regard him warily. She closed her eyes for a second and when she opened them again—damn, was that a trace of tears? Her knuckles tensed around the baby monitor. "It mattered to me." And she disappeared into the house.

It had mattered to him, too. But as much as he knew he was special to her, that could never match the craving he had to matter the most.

To completely belong to each other.

Chapter Six

Cadie eyed the clock over the mirrored wall in the PT area and cringed. Zach would arrive for his Monday appointment in ten minutes and she hadn't figured out how to address her embarrassing overreaction from Saturday. Why had she freaked out? Calling her Cadie just lumped him in with the rest of the world.

I wanted to be different...

And she'd liked that he was. A fact of which he was now well aware. Things would be even *more* awkward. Holding in some choice cusses, she rubbed disinfectant onto the handle of a treadmill hard enough to make the whole thing shake.

"Mutti, heute morgen."

Zach's voice, always a little jarring when speaking to his mom in German because Cadie had zero frame of reference for the language, drifted in from the reception area. Her back stiffened. So much for a ten-minute reprieve. Rushing to fold the cloth and hang it on the towel rack she—fine, she *and* Lauren—had installed on the wall, she brushed her hands down her tank top and pasted on a smile in preparation. Maybe if she didn't bring Saturday up, he'd follow suit? She'd left him hanging in the backyard and by the time she'd come downstairs with Ben, he'd disappeared.

He emerged around the glass-block wall and—

Holy crap, he was using a cane, not crutches. Joy sang in her chest. Her fake smile turned real and she had to hold herself back from cheering in deference to the cell phone he held to his ear.

"*Ja, ich bin sehr glücklich…* I know, *Mutti…* Yeah, put him on." Zach sent Cadie an apologetic look and mouthed *sorry* as he leaned against the wall nearest the treadmills. He wore different workout clothes from his morning appointment—a navy, wicking T-shirt and a pair of soccer shorts. "Papa, hey… *Si, veinticinco horas por semana…*"

Cadie normally loved listening to Zach talk to his parents on the phone. His seamless transitions between German, English and Spanish—French, too, if he felt like it—made her feel like she was standing in the concourse at the UN headquarters or something. According to Zach, his parents insisted on speaking their native languages to their kids because they wanted to keep Zach and his sisters from getting rusty. And for Cadie…well, there was something about his voice, plus rapid Spanish…

She moved over to the weight rack and busied herself lining up the dumbbells and medicine balls.

"*En octubre yo vendré por una semana… Marisol debería venir en diciembre. Sutter Creek no abrirá antes de Whistler.*"

Yeah. *That* something. She only caught the meaning of every third word—something about a week in October and his sister, Marisol, and December—but the content wasn't what turned her insides gooey. To borrow Tavish's favorite phrase, holy hell.

A pair of strong arms wrapped around her from behind. The two small dumbbells she'd been moving landed on the rack with a clatter. "Zach!"

"That's from my mother." His hands settled on her shoulders. "You're jumpy today."

She turned, ignoring his obvious statement lest she admit she was sensitive to his touch, not the surprise. "You have a cane! That's awesome."

He grinned. "Right? And the doctor's allowing me to increase my hours at work—twenty-five a week."

"Ah, I thought you mentioned something like that to your dad, but it's been far too long since I sat in Señora Vargas's class and studied my ass off for a pitiful C."

His eyes glinted. "You just had the wrong teacher."

Oh, Lord. Okay. That bordered on flirting. His good mood clearly nullified any awkwardness on his part. And she'd take it, run with the possibility that all wasn't lost. They were making excellent progress with his therapy. If they could make it to the end of today's appointment without the space between them snapping like an electrical storm, Monday would have exceeded her expectations.

"You know," Zach gasped an hour later after completing a set of sprints on the recumbent bike, "I think it's unfair to take our 'business only' deal out on the bottom line of the people we know and love. Nora was probably confused when she didn't see us in her diner for lunch the past couple Fridays."

Cadie plunked down sideways on the seat of the bike next to him, looking downright edible in a tennis-style skirt and tank top. He'd have thought he'd be immune to her in work clothes by now, but nope. Heat curled in his belly as he watched her skirt ride up. She fiddled with the settings on his bike to make them easier and shrugged. "Given you've taken a huge step today, don't you think we should stick with what works?"

Sucking up his disappointment that she wasn't letting him push to the limit on the bike, he focused on her clear lack of enthusiasm. "Exactly. A huge step. We deserve a celebration. I'll take you out for dinner."

Her head snapped up and her gaze met his. "You think that's a good idea? Losing focus now…"

"Come on, Cadence. Getting off the sticks is a big deal. Work with me here." He couldn't exactly say why it mattered so much for her to agree, but it did. He wanted to believe that once their agreement was over they could go back to normal.

"But Ben…" she said weakly.

"All the better. Not hanging out with you means not getting to snuggle my godson."

The smallest twist formed between her brows. "I already have groceries. We'd probably have enough if you wanted to join us."

"Nope. Not good enough. As much as I enjoy dinner at your place, I feel like celebrating."

She deflated a little. "Justified. You've worked hard."

"So have you."

"Just doing my job."

Man, he wanted to take his thumb and smooth out the wrinkle in her forehead. He rubbed his hand along his thigh instead. Her continued resistance dragged out his competitive instinct. A lightbulb went off. The Sutter Creek Founder's Day festivities—fireworks, live music, a children's festival—started Friday afternoon. "Friday, then."

She drummed the pads of her fingers on her knees. "Friday?"

"Yes. Celebratory picnic—Ben'll love it. And then he can sleep in his stroller while we watch the fireworks."

Three weeks ago she wouldn't have thought twice about joining him for a picnic. But the long blink of those long eyelashes said, *That's a borderline date.* She must have read the writing on the wall, or rather, the desire written on his face.

But then why had she touched him like she had on Saturday? Delving her fingers into his hair, an innocent attempt to unwind his muscles that had left his need for her a knotted rope, tangled in his feet, tripping him up. Second-guessing decisions he never would have doubted before. Keeping his emotions unfrayed had been possible when he'd been certain he was the sole person aware of them. But even if she had figured him out, he couldn't let that stop him from following through on his promises to Sam. So until she told him to clear out of her life, she was stuck with him.

He pedaled lazy circles and waited for her response… Maybe a *Yeah, sure, Zach. I can keep ignoring the way you check out my legs when you think I'm not looking…* or *what part of* no *do you not understand, jackass?*

When she finally answered it was a much less complicated affair.

"Friday…" she mused.

"That a yes or a no?"

"It's a 'do everything I say this week and I'll consider it.'"

Nodding, he mentally prepped himself to follow her instructions. If only his crotch followed the rules as well as his brain.

* * *

On Friday afternoon Zach slumped on a weight bench in the physio office doing his best wrung-out dish towel impression. "All right, General Grigg," he said to Cadie, "how'd I do with following instructions?"

"Hmm?" she said absently as she typed on her phone. They were alone in the facility and she was splitting her attention between monitoring him and replying to a handful of end-of-the-week emails she'd apologized profusely for having to deal with.

"Doing everything you said this week," he paraphrased. Their conversation from Monday was still fresh in his head despite him trying his best to think about things other than taking her to the Founder's Day fireworks. "Did I check all the boxes?"

"Well, how's your pain?"

"Minimal." When he was stationary, at least.

"Stand in front of me," she commanded, a small twitch playing at the corner of her mouth.

Impatience rose in his chest but he complied. Routine had carried him through the last four workdays. Eat, physio, eat, work, physio and then dinner, until he collapsed into bed for a solid eight hours. Going into work for a short shift every day, even if he was still limited to basic site supervision, had been a breath of fresh air, literally and figuratively. And now he wanted his damned reward. An evening where he could still pretend that his attraction to Cadie—his feelings for her—hadn't thrown an industrial-size wrench into their friendship.

She studied him. Clinical, that gaze. The careful eye of a professional looking for minor imbalances.

"Like what you see?"

Surprise flashed across her face. "Uh, well…"

Nicely done, champ. He rushed to cover up his unintentional innuendo. "I meant muscularly."

Ah, man. That wasn't much better.

"Muscles. Right. Well, yours are—" She cleared her throat and muttered a word that she only used when her son wasn't around. "Looking pretty good tonight." She cringed. "Uh, balanced."

"I know what you mean." Sending her a sheepish smile, he brushed a thumb down her blushing cheek. "Let me buy you and Ben dinner. We can watch the fireworks together. You've done as much as I have, here—you deserve a night off."

An awkward tilt marred her smile. "If you throw in mini donuts, you've got a deal."

This is only to celebrate. He doesn't want anything more.

Cadie spread a blanket on the lawn of Sutter Creek's currently bustling, grassy Main Street Square and ignored her jittering stomach. She didn't want Zach to want more. Yeah, sure, being desired had its charms, but the emotional cost of falling for someone again? No, thank you.

"I'm annexing your blanket," the man in question announced, snagging a giggling Ben and gently roughhousing with him. Holy crap, Zach looked good tonight. A black T-shirt hugged his chest, just tight enough to make her mouth water but not so fitted that he looked like he'd stolen clothes off a gym rat. His muted-color plaid shorts hung low on his hips, and when he hoisted Ben high in the air, his T-shirt rode up, exposing a lickable slice of skin.

Talk about Sahara Desert mouth.

Instead of focusing her pathetic lack of mental self-control when it came to Zach and his rippling obliques, she watched her son as he squealed with delight at the airplane ride. Big man plus small kid, and both of them sporting grins—so sweet.

Her heart flipped over. That wasn't any better than getting turned on by a flash of Zach's bronze-skinned stomach.

Scanning the site rapidly for something, anything, to look at that didn't involve Zach Cardenas, she spotted a number of familiar faces, including Lauren and Tavish, who sat snuggled on a blanket of their own near the gazebo that centered the square. She waved at them frantically. They waved back and started to cross the lawn. Maybe if they came over, she'd be less inclined to leave puddles of drool on the blanket.

He lifted Ben again and her professional instincts kicked in. She didn't want him to re-injure his arm and make it difficult for him to use his cane. "He's too heavy for you, Zach."

"He's a feather, Cadence," he said, tucking and rolling onto his back with Ben along for the ride. "My arm is healed. I promise, it's completely comfortable to lift him. I wouldn't, otherwise. I'm not going to drop your kid."

"I wasn't worried about that. I just—"

"You're just overprotective," Lauren announced, plunking herself down on the blanket and sitting cross-legged. Tavish lounged behind her, lying propped up on one elbow and snugging Lauren against his torso.

"If she is, it's because I deserve it," Zach said.

Lauren arched a blond brow. "Misbehaving?"

Cadie wished. After all his time on the freestyle skiing circuit, Zach probably had an excellent list of ways to misbehave. A shriek of joy from Ben saved her from having to answer.

"Nephew hog." Lauren leaned over to Zach, arms outstretched. "My turn."

"A-ti!"

"And uncle," Tavish added.

Cadie filled her lungs with warm, evening air. Yes. This was good. Zach had adjusted his shirt so it hung over the waistband of his shorts again, her sister and Tavish were providing conversation—

"Garnet told me you're looking to start dating," Lauren announced.

Cadie hadn't known it was possible to choke on air but she somehow managed it, coughing enough that Zach gave her a couple of good whacks on the back.

Once she had her breath back, she glared at him. "Has it been that long since you last did first aid, genius? You're not supposed to pound a choking person on the back."

His expression went Pinot Grigio dry. "Well aware. But there wasn't anything in your airway."

Yes, there had been—her shock that her sister would bring up what should have been a sensitive, girls-only topic. She shifted her glare to Lauren, a silent *what the hell* challenge.

Lauren kissed the top of Ben's head and widened her eyes, the fakest innocence Cadie had seen since Lauren tried to cover up the dent she'd put in their father's car back in high school.

"What? We're all family here," her sister said.

And if Cadie refused to talk about it at all, either Zach would figure out that his presence was complicating the topic or, even worse, Lauren would figure that out. Though Lauren *had* subtly suggested not too long ago that she suspected Zach was interested in Cadie. Given that, why would she bring up Cadie dating in front of him?

Unless she wanted to push... *No.* Cadie wasn't going to traverse that dark, brambly trail.

"Cadie? Was Garnet totally off base?" Lauren pressed, lying Ben down on his back and taking off his sandals so that she could play This Little Piggy with his toes.

Cadie bit her lip. Talking about *potentially* dating didn't mean she'd actually *have to* date. Actually, if Zach thought she was interested in dating, it could cover how much she wanted to strip him down and eat him for dessert. Guaranteed nothing in the picnic basket he'd lugged over could compare to the taste of his skin.

"I, uh, I guess I'd be interested? Maybe?"

Zach's face darkened and Cadie's heart sank. Did he not think she should date? That it was too soon since Sam?

"Super casually," she tacked on.

His frown didn't budge.

Annoyance flared in her chest. Now she kind of wanted to go on a date, just to prove that, though she appreciated all his help and support, said help and support didn't give him a say in her social life. "What? You don't think I should?"

He blinked, shaking his head. "It's been over a year. I don't think it would be unusual to think of seeing people."

"I think it's a good idea," Lauren said loyally, squeaking as her fiancé poked her in the side.

"Business and minding and all that, sweetheart," Tavish said.

"Sisters and you-don't-get-it and all that, *sweetheart*," Lauren retorted.

"Look," Cadie said, "as much as I think it's awesome that everyone has an opinion on my love life—"

"None from me, Cades," Tavish interrupted.

She cocked a brow at him. "I'll adjust that, then. As

much as the two of you—" she eyed a smirking Lauren and a flat-mouthed Zach "—need to follow in Tavish's superiorly intelligent footsteps—"

"See, Pixie? Superiorly intelligent. At least one Dawson understands my brillia—" Tavish groaned as Lauren elbowed him in the gut.

"Keep interrupting me and I'll withdraw the compliment," Cadie teased. "And I'll date when I'm ready, Lauren."

Lauren's face scrunched.

Cadie caught another frown from Zach. His hand, lying on the blanket, was in the corner of her field of vision, though, and it flexed into a fist. "Really, it's not a big deal," she said. "It is what it is."

Zach sat up and shifted closer to her. He started stroking a soothing rhythm along her spine. The breath shuddered from her lungs. She could pretend the emptiness at her core was grief. But nope. It was because this was all they'd ever have, small comforts between friends.

That was *not* enough.

Nor was it at all okay that she felt that way.

"I don't know if you're expected to ever feel fully ready," he murmured.

The temptation to lean into his hand pulled at her. No way, though. Lauren would for sure notice and would redouble her campaign to get Cadie to admit to wanting things that would never be. It would be safer to just agree to a date. "I was talking to Garnet about the *possibility* of dating. I'm pretty busy, though."

Zach withdrew his fingers and Cadie's spine gave a little sob.

Lauren shifted her gaze to Zach. "Who's single in the search-and-rescue circles these days?"

A strangled noise creaked from Zach's gaping mouth.

"I'm not dating some rando SAR dude," Cadie said, mouthing an unmistakable curse at Lauren before focusing on riffling through the diaper bag for the container of Ben's fishy crackers. What was the word for murdering one's sister again? Sororicide?

Lauren snapped her fingers. "Isn't the doctor who replaced me at the clinic single? What's his name? Caleb? And you know him, Cadie, so that would take away some of the awkward."

"I know *of* him. He was Sam's friend, not mine. We never hung out." Caleb Matsuda had been a ski buddy to both Sam and Zach back in Colorado, and had been one of the other people caught in the avalanche that killed Sam. She'd only run into him once since he moved to Sutter Creek a couple of weeks ago, and he'd been vague about his reasons for the change. Maybe he had something in common with Cadie, needed to rebuild after the avalanche. But seriously? Dating him?

Staring at her sister, trying to figure out if pregnancy hormones had stolen all of Lauren's sense, Cadie shook her head. "Bit of baggage there, Laur."

Ben, who'd been on hands and knees examining the grass as if it was the most fascinating thing in the world—probably was to an almost-one-year-old—crawled over to Cadie, held up his arms and demanded, "Mama!" She enveloped her son in a hug and breathed in the still-a-baby scent that clung to his blond hair. The fragrance soothed better than any of the aromatherapy techniques Garnet practiced at the clinic.

The corners of Lauren's mouth turned down. "Too much baggage?"

"Probably." She'd have too much baggage for any man. But she didn't want to cop to her fears. "Hey, Tavish, have you fully moved out of Mackenzie's apartment?"

He nodded. "Left a lot of my furniture—didn't have room for it at the house. But all my personal belongings are out."

"Do you know if Kenz has rented it out yet?"

"Don't think so. All she cares about at the moment is trying to get half a night's solid sleep."

Cadie winced. "Been there." Glancing up at Zach, she acknowledged he'd been the one to keep her sane through those early months of parenthood. He smiled back and lifted a shoulder as if to say, "Any time."

Ugh, why did he have to check so many boxes aside from hot-as-hell? Shaking her head, she pushed forward. "If Kenz is willing, I want to rent her place."

Lauren's jaw dropped. "And leave Dad's?"

"I figure it's time."

"I thought you had a good give-and-take roommate system going on."

"We do," Cadie said carefully. "And it's been a bonus to be able to watch over him since his heart episode. But he's doing way better. And…" Oof, how to say it? She didn't want to sound callous. Didn't want to minimize the times grief still washed over her. But she only had to deal with the occasional rogue wave now, not the constant undertow.

"And so are you," Zach offered. "Doing way better, that is."

She blinked, startled by the simplicity of his statement. By the fact it was sometimes true. "Getting there, anyway."

Popping her lips, Lauren tilted her head. "Yeah, I can pick up any slack when it comes to Dad—" Tavish cleared his throat meaningfully and Lauren leaned further against him and squeezed his knee. "Within reason, Tav."

"Dad really doesn't need much help anymore," Cadie said. "He's back to cooking some nights. Antsy to get back to work full-time."

"It sucks being off," Zach muttered from his reclined position. He held his arms out to Ben, who crawled over and, thumb in mouth, draped himself over Zach.

"It sucks going back to work full-time and never healing properly, too," Cadie said, managing to insert enough disapproval into her voice to cover the way her heart was panging. The bond between her son and this good, strong man never failed to melt her. And there was plenty of room for her to nuzzle Zach, too, right into the notch at the base of his neck. Let the outdoors-and-soap smell of him get stuck in her nose and on her skin and—

"Let us know if you need help moving," Lauren said, saving Cadie before the heat in her belly started to show on her face.

Chapter Seven

"He's asleep," Cadie called from the patio as she approached Zach, the soles of her flip-flops crunching along the gravel path that edged her lawn. He kept his eyes closed. The chirp of crickets and the sway of the cushioned backyard swing lulled him, reminding him he'd been up at six and had barely sat down since. Sure, they'd technically been relaxing during their picnic earlier in the evening. But the minute Lauren had brought up Cadie dating, it set Cadie off. And when she got tense, he followed.

Her footsteps halted close to him and the seat jolted as she sat. "Sorry about Ben's freak-out. I know you wanted to watch the fireworks."

Rolling his head to the side on the back of the swing, he smiled. Not the first time he'd had his plans changed by Ben. Couldn't predict the needs of a baby. "We'll see some of them from here." The Dawson house sat on a ridge overlooking the golf course and had a decent view of the base of the mountain. They'd miss anything low down, but the exciting stuff would be visible above the trees and neighborhoods sandwiched between the fairways and the ski lifts.

"Sleepy?" she asked.

"Yeah."

"You should go home. And sleep in tomorrow. No work, no PT...what'll you do with yourself?"

"Try out the new bike trail cut off Devil's Playground? Andrew says it's a thrill." He opened his eyes and blinked at her. Flags of color rose on her cheeks in the dim, half light from the crescent moon and the strand of round, decorative bulbs hanging from between two pines behind them.

Scoffing, she dropped her flip-flops off her feet and tucked her legs sideways. Her knees rested an inch from his thigh. If he shifted, they'd be touching. Corralling the groan clamoring to escape, he stretched his arms along the back of the seat. One more body part now within an inch of her. *Smart move, Cardenas.*

"Sorry about my sister. I don't know what got into her tonight."

"Standard sibling matter, Cadence. I have three. I know the drill."

"Yeah, you would." She chuckled. The cotton of her sweatshirt stretched over her breasts as she crossed her arms.

Each a perfect handful...? He gulped. "Most of my life my dad and I were the unwilling tube riders being dragged behind the family boat as my mom and sisters drove."

A laugh broke from her chest, full and genuine and accompanied by a gorgeous smile. Man, when was the last time he'd heard her laugh like that? Had he, since Sam died? He couldn't remember.

And damn, he could go for being the one to coax that sound out again.

The joyous noise trailed off and her brows knitted. "What?"

"Huh?"

"You're staring."

"I was just enjoying—" Best not finish that. No need to draw attention to how she was far more serious now than before she'd been widowed. "Uh… At least Lauren's not treating you like glass anymore."

"Yeah." A serious look passed through her eyes, dark in the muted light. "Everyone seems to have some wise opinion concerning me and dating."

Oh, he had an opinion about her dating, all right. But it was the antithesis of wise. No matter how much they wanted to, the words "date me" were not going to come out of his mouth. Nor was he going to play the jerk wad "I can't have you so no one can" game. "You'll do what you need to do when it's time to do it."

A snort shook her slim frame. "Smartest thing I've heard all day."

"Glad I could help," he muttered. It didn't make sense. He'd thought she'd figured out his interest in her, hence her getting all awkward. But if she knew he wanted her, why did she keep poking at him? Unless she didn't know? But he'd been so sure—

"You know, these last few weeks have shown me that if I'm going to have the life I want, I need to come out of the grief fog I've been hiding in."

His throat went tight. "Yeah?"

Her gaze darted to his sandaled feet, which he was rocking back and forth to keep the swing in motion. "If I don't call on you for help as much, I don't want to hurt your feelings. I'm not, am I?"

"Nah." Zach swallowed. He'd only promised to be there for Cadie when she needed him. He hadn't really contemplated what it would feel like when they'd got to the stage where she wouldn't. And it ate at him. "Good to know how you feel. Honesty's important, right?"

"Honesty's crucial. I didn't have enough of that with Sam. Didn't tell him how I felt as much as I should have. Maybe he would have done things differently had I voiced my fears."

Zach covered up his wince with a nod. Cadie could have taken out full-page ads in the Steamboat Springs's newspaper and Sam wouldn't have done things differently. But badmouthing the dead wasn't Zach's style. His mom would string him up by her rosary if she heard him even *thinking* ill of Sam, let alone vocalizing his doubts.

"I dunno, Cadie," he said. Now that he'd broken the seal on the nickname, it was slipping out more often. "Playing the 'could have done' game probably isn't healthy. But continuing to be more open with your sister will be."

"I'm trying. So is she—she's more aware—but she doesn't really listen all the time, you know? She looks at me like some sort of wounded person—her physician instincts kick in too much."

She reached across her body to lay her hand on the elbow of the arm he still had extended on the seat. A thrill rippled along his skin and he sucked in a slow breath to suppress the pleasure.

"What about you?" she said. "Pretty sure you play the what-if game, too."

The hint of guilt in her eyes wrecked him. Did she need to hear his doubts? She'd still never asked about the night before the avalanche, and he'd promised not to tell her until she asked. And he clung to the excuse not to tell her about the argument he'd had with Sam. But he couldn't completely hide his regrets.

"I still wonder if things would have been different had I been part of the filming that day," he said. "Him having you, and Ben not being born yet… It'll never feel fair."

"You could say that."

They'd had variations on this conversation a number of times over the past year. And her continued lashed-to-the-past mindset made his heart ache. She had nothing to feel guilty about.

Not like him.

"Cadence, for all that it won't feel fair, Sam will always be part of your life—mine, too. You don't have to carry his death as a burden."

"But our relationship was so undone when he died. How am I supposed to move forward when everything with Sam was one giant loose end?"

"I don't know." He could tie that loose end up for her. Yeah, Sam's final moments had been filled with love and remorse and ensuring Ben and Cadie were taken care of, not with discussions about divorce and anger. Zach hadn't put much stock in the whole "deathbed conversion" thing until he'd seen Sam go through it. And Zach clung to that, wanted to think the best of the man who he'd considered his closest friend for years. Because the night prior, Sam's words had been very different. *I'm not going to be able to love this baby.* Would it help or hinder Cadie to know that before Sam had asked for Zach's vow to support her and Ben, he'd made it clear he didn't want to be a father?

How on earth was Zach supposed to relay the answer to the mystery she was searching for without devastating her? He shifted, resting his palm between her shoulder blades. Not so much as to drape his arm over her shoulders—that seemed too forward. But the anguish pulling at the corners of her mouth demanded physical comfort.

Her body heat seeped through her sweatshirt as he trailed his hand from her upper back to her waist. She inched closer, tucking against his side with her knee resting against his thigh.

His heart filled to brimming, warming his chest. The quiet space of time, curled up in the semi-darkness…

With my best friend's widow. I am such a lowlife.

She seemed to want the closeness, though. And he lacked the strength to deny her.

The initial crackle and boom of fireworks split the silence and they soaked in the mesmerizing flashes of light. Cadie's breathing was calm, even, in complete opposition to Zach's racing heart. How was he supposed to be chill when he had everything he ever wanted fitted in his one-armed embrace? When she rested her head on his shoulder and the faint fragrance of cherries and sugar drifted over the aroma of pine sap coming off the trees behind them?

I'm relishing this too much. But for once, he ignored the self-recrimination. Tightened his arm around the woman. As long as he didn't label his feelings, he could pretend it wasn't as bad as he knew it to be. Dropping a kiss to the top of her head, he focused on the rainbow bursts in the sky and the sweet weight of holding Cadie.

After ten minutes the pace of the blasts picked up, a cascade of white showers filling the sky.

Cadie sighed happily. She moved a hand to his thigh and traced small circles. He wore twill cargo shorts, but the fairly thick material felt thin as a tissue beneath her touch. His leg lit up like the final blitz of pyrotechnics illuminating the dark sky. Suppressing a groan, he shifted in the seat.

"Pretty," Cadie said. "Good show this year."

"Yeah," he croaked.

She sat up so she wasn't under his arm anymore. But her bent legs still rested against his. His head swam with her sweet scent.

She stared at his mouth. A flicker of resistance crossed her face, battling something way too close to arousal for his willpower to handle.

"Zach…"

He brushed a palm along her cheek. She closed her eyes and leaned into the gesture.

Oh.

That was…unexpected.

And he couldn't move his hand away for the life of him. Nor could he stop himself from stroking his thumb closer to her mouth. So close. Too close.

She parted her lips.

Damn.

Just one touch…

The callus on his thumb caught a little as he traced the sexy-soft skin of her lower lip.

The rise of her chin served as an unmistakable invitation.

Oh, yeah. Brilliant. He stilled his thumb on the corner of her perfect, tempting mouth. "Cadie…"

Her chin lifted another degree.

And his self-control bottomed out. Groaning, he leaned in, testing the softness of those lips with his own instead of with his hand.

The thudding of his heart replaced the now quiet fireworks, a rapid beat in his ears. Their mouths met—gentle presses and nips and the faintest taste of vanilla from her breath.

More. Need clamored in his belly. He ran his tongue

along the plump flesh of her bottom lip. She whimpered, froze for a second, but then opened for him. Her fingers scrambled for purchase on his shoulders and neck, and she delved a hand into his hair, pulling him closer, further under her spell.

More... Yeah right. He could try to slake his desire with a few moments of savoring her mouth.

But as if he'd ever get enough of Cadence.

Wow... *Wow*, could Zach Cardenas kiss. His firm lips molded to Cadie's, leading her with the rhythm of a ballroom dancer, accepting her fumbling steps in return. Heat spread through her body like wildfire. His work-worn palm scraped deliciously against her cheek. The fingers of his other hand played an irresistible rhythm along her spine. And his taste... Masculine. Sexy as hell.

A moan escaped her throat as his tongue dueled with hers.

You knew kissing him would be good.

Kissing him.

Kissing *Zach*.

Her conscience sloshed a bucket of cold water over her brain.

Tearing her mouth away, her hands from his hard, strong body, she scrambled back until she collided with the arm of the swing. Her quick motion sent the seat rocking.

Staring at her, he raised a hand to his open mouth and slowly rubbed his lips. The ambient light from the strand of outdoor bulbs glinted in the sheen of passion that was turning his green eyes almost black.

What have we done?

Was she *trying* to lose him? Nausea licked at the back of her throat. Would admitting she was worried about losing their friendship push them in that very direction? She scrambled for some other reason to classify their kiss as an egregious mistake. *Work.* She could blame work. She didn't even need to call it an excuse. Her code of ethics was exceedingly clear on therapist-client relations. "We shouldn't have done that."

He dropped his hand to the back of the seat. The skin of his knuckles strained as he gripped the top of the cushion. "I'm—"

"Don't apologize," she snapped. "It's my fault. You're my client. I know better."

His brow furrowed. "We're friends first, Cadence."

"We sure aren't acting like it." She'd nearly crawled in his lap tonight, for heaven's sake. For a few long minutes she'd let her loneliness take over, had pretended nothing stood in the way of her attraction to this man.

Playing pretend is for children and fools.

Sitting sideways on the seat, she brought her tucked legs to her chest, wrapped her arms around her shins and dropped her forehead to her knees. *Breathe.* After a few rhythmic inhalations and exhalations, she fixed him with what she hoped was a firm but apologetic expression. "You're going to have to go back to your other therapist. I can't work with you now that this happened."

His shoulders stiffened. "No."

"Zach, I can't risk my practice—"

"You're not."

Panic clamped around her throat. "We kissed!"

"Yeah, I was there," he said wryly.

"How can you be so calm about this?"

A flicker of disbelief lit his eyes and he wiped a hand down his face. Okay. So he wasn't calm. He was just better at hiding it. "I've made more progress with you over the past few weeks than I had in a few months.

And half the SAR volunteers have signed up for your center's services since opening day. Don't get me wrong, I'm not taking all the credit for that, but I do think my word of mouth made some difference," he said. "So between my therapy and you wanting to build your business, neither of us can afford to go back on our deal."

"But you—" Tears pricked the corners of her eyes and she blinked them away. He'd mentioned honesty was important earlier. Well, he was going to get some honesty. She had to make him see how stupid it would be for them to keep working together. "I'm attracted to you, Zach. Which was one thing when I was hiding it, but now that you know—"

His beautiful mouth, the one her lips clamored to kiss just one more time, fell open. "How long have you been hiding it?"

"Months! Why do you think things were so freaking awkward between us?"

"I thought—" He brushed his hand along his mouth again. "I thought you'd figured *me* out."

"Figured out *what*?"

"I've wanted to kiss you for a long time."

Ask him how long. But his teeth, toying at the lower lip she still craved the taste of, set off warning bells. Did she want to know the answer?

"Okay," she said, voice shaking. "So we're both attracted to each other. Just normal human biology."

"Right," he said on a laugh. "Science. Nothing beyond a few ill-advised hormones."

"This is not funny."

He shook his head. "It's a little funny."

She glared at him.

"Look," he said. "We're adults. I'm sure we both have a list of reasons why acting on our attraction would be a bad idea. Maybe now that we know how we both feel, it'll be easier to resist."

"Ever the optimist."

"Maybe. But I'm not risking being ready for my trip to Whistler because I lost sense for a second and kissed you."

Goose bumps rose on her arms despite her hoodie and she rubbed them, trying to get rid of the neural reflex. "It's right in my association's rule book, though. No sexual relationships."

"Fair. And I'm betting there's some stuff about positions of power and whatever. But one kiss is not a sexual relationship. And I was the one who kissed you—"

"But I—"

Irritation crossed his face. "*I* kissed *you*. You're my friend's widow and I *kissed* you. I think that's the bigger sin here, Cadie. So forgive me if I'm persistent, okay? I have to get this film done. I *promised*."

Well, crap. What did it say about her that Sam hadn't even factored into her guilt? But it clearly did for Zach. Not surprising. Honor mattered to him. And given she was at fault for tarnishing his, she wasn't going to be the one to stop him from cleaning it up. "Fine. I'll keep you on my client list. But no more of this."

No kissing him again. The chagrined shadow that crossed Zach's handsome face wasn't enough to quell the disappointment stabbing through her core.

Chapter Eight

The road from Bozeman seemed long with endless possibilities as Zach piloted his truck along the winding asphalt that hugged the Gallatin River. At least he had some good news to interject into the all-business dialogue that had dominated his interactions with Cadie since they'd kissed two and a half weeks ago. The Sutter Creek hospital wasn't a major center, so other than emergencies, specialists needed to be seen out of town. He'd gone into Bozeman for a Tuesday checkup with his orthopedic surgeon—walked into the office with his cane.

And exited with his hands free for the first time since April.

Exhilaration buoyed him. A good chunk of the weight that had sat on his shoulders since his accident fell away.

The clock on the dash read three in the afternoon. Freedom tasted like a beer-and-a-burger special in the lounge of the Sutter Creek Hotel. And he'd see if his buddies were up for a post-work gathering. But first he had to find Cadie to tell her that all their hard work had paid off.

Fifteen minutes later he strolled into Evolve's foyer.

Lauren waved at him from behind the front counter. "You're missing something!"

He held up his palms and gave her some solid jazz hands on his way to the physiotherapy suite. "Look, Mom, no cane!"

She grinned. "Brilliant. You here to find my sister?"

He paused in front of the frosted-glass door. "Yeah."

"She's off early. Went for a coffee at Peak Beans."

"Which shop? Main Street or the lodge?"

Lauren's gaze darted to a point behind the desk. "Main."

Walking over to the counter, he leaned an elbow on the reclaimed-wood surface. "Think she's up for an interruption?"

She nodded. "Don't see why not."

He sent her a questioning look. Something about her expression reminded him of when his sisters tried to pull the wool over his eyes when they were kids. "You sure?"

"Mmm-hmm."

She sounded anything but. However, Zach wasn't in the mood to overanalyze. Lauren must have detected Zach and Cadie's new system: eyes down, never talk about their mutual attraction. And his additional step: hope to hell Cadie had bought his agreement about it just being physical chemistry.

Lauren coughed. "How's the film going?"

"Fine. Other than the trip to the site to get my reflections, I'm mostly done with my part." Back when he was hampered by a broken leg and arm, he'd offered the film's editing department his labor. Last week he'd sent them what he had. He was happy to be rid of the task—watching old clips of Sam and knowing he'd kissed Sam's wife hadn't done much for the guilt permanently singeing his stomach lining. Nor had the few extra sessions in the gym helped clear his mind of Cadie's lips on his. Any time he stepped onto exercise equipment, the echo of her gentle corrections lingered on his skin.

"Still planning for Whistler in October?"

"Yeah, month and a half to go." He clapped his hands together once. "And I need to tell your sister that we can now get serious about getting me in shape for the back-country."

Lauren's smile went falsely guileless again. "Say hi for me."

Cadie sipped her iced latte, and tried to forget about all the things she could be crossing off her to-do list this afternoon. Her tablemate smiled at her and lifted his own drink to his lips. Hopefully he was oblivious to the fact she was thinking about the moving boxes scattered around her bedroom.

She'd asked Caleb Matsuda out for coffee to get Lauren off her back. And she couldn't complain about spending an hour enjoying his stellar smile and the way his stylish button-down showed off his fit physique. But it was an objective enjoyment. Her stomach was perfectly settled; her heart beat a slow, calm rhythm. Too bad. Had she been looking for a relationship, Caleb would have skewed to the favorable side of a pro-con list. Good job, outdoorsy, claimed to like kids…

"How old is Ben now?" he asked, ruffling his hand through his short, dark brown hair.

"Turns one this month. It's gone slowly and quickly all at the same time."

"My mom always says the days go slow and the years go fast."

She nodded. Her chest panged that she'd never get similar advice from her own mom, having lost her to cancer when Cadie was twelve. She had her father, though. If she turned out to be half the parent her dad was, she'd be doing okay. "Wise lady. My dad says something similar."

"You're close to your family, then," he said.

"Yeah, I've actually been living with my dad since I returned home. But I'm moving out this weekend, into my sister-in-law's old place," she blurted, trying to salvage some semblance of adulthood. "Why I thought it was a good idea to move, with the clinic still brand-new and Ben's first birthday party happening in a couple weeks, I don't know, but I latched onto the idea and couldn't let it go. And I wasn't sure how my dad would take it, but he seems almost happy at the prospect of being on his own again. He—" Her face warmed. "I'm sorry, I'm rambling."

Caleb smiled and his eyes twinkled. "No problem. I'm glad you're doing well."

She and Caleb had run the gamut of other topics— hobbies, work, things to do in Sutter Creek given he'd just moved to town. Prior to meeting him at Sam's funeral, she hadn't known him well. But the avalanche now connected him to Cadie in an odd, indelible way. She knew something intensely personal about him without knowing much else.

He didn't press further about her family, so she returned the query. "What about you?"

"My parents are in New York. Brooklyn. Both doctors. Thrilled I followed in their footsteps. Not so much that I'm practicing 2000 miles away from them." He smiled, a flash of straight, white teeth. She waited for his clean-shaved jaw and the glint of humor in his eye to melt her insides into molten heat.

Nope. Nothing.

A jolt of frustration hit her. A mere two seconds in Zach's presence turned her on. Why not with Caleb? Not that she wanted to be with someone, but it would be nice to get a flicker of attraction to another man.

She poked at the ice cubes in her coffee with a wooden stir stick. "What made you leave Denver? I thought you were some hot-shot surgeon there."

He lifted a shoulder. "I needed a change of scenery."

"Didn't want to go back home?"

"New York moves at an even faster clip than Denver. I wanted to try something completely different. Quiet."

Safe. He didn't say it, but she read it in his eyes. The avalanche had been no small trauma. "Sutter Creek is that. If you want it to be."

"Cadie." He ringed his thumbs and fingers around his coffee cup. "Did you ask me out for coffee because you wanted to talk about Sam—" his tone thickened "—or the avalanche? Or…something else?"

I wanted to pretend for two seconds that someone other than Zach could catch my eye.

Yeah, that was going to stay in her inside voice. And she wasn't going to admit to her childish need to thumb her nose at her sister. "I'm not sure. But I think…"

"It's too soon?"

She smiled gratefully for the out.

The bell on the door chimed and Caleb's dark brows drew together. "Isn't Zach still using his cane?"

"Yeah," she said, turning, "the last time I che—"

Her throat closed over.

Zach didn't have his cane anymore. But the look of joy he'd worn when he'd downgraded from his crutches was nowhere to be seen. Gray tinged his complexion and he was rubbing his jaw as if he had an abscessed tooth. His gaze flitted from Caleb to Cadie and back to Caleb, and his lips flattened as he dropped his hand to his side.

She waved him over. And she didn't like the look of

his gait. For someone who was no longer using a walking aid, he still held a trace of a limp. If that was the case, the doctor really shouldn't have—

"You sure you should have given up the crutches, man? If anyone knows you can't rush healing, it's me." Caleb said, holding up a hand. For the first time, Cadie noticed a network of surgical scars on his palm and wrist. Right, he'd hurt his hand badly in the avalanche. Maybe that partly explained his career change.

Caleb's smile dimmed as his gaze locked on Cadie. He stuck his hand in his lap.

Heat ran up her cheeks. "Sorry, didn't mean to stare. I'd forgotten... Never mind," she said, waving for Zach to join them. Zach raked both his hands through his chestnut hair. The sleeves of his T-shirt rode up his arms, exposing the cut line of his biceps... *Oh, Lord.*

"I'm not staying," he said. "I just wanted to pass along an update from my doctor. He's cleared me for full activity as my strength allows. But you're busy, so I'll—"

"Okay, so that's great news," she said. "And, uh, how'd you know where to find me?"

"Lauren."

What the hell? She blinked in confusion. Her sister had known she was out for coffee with Caleb. Had encouraged the date, no less. So why was Lauren sending Zach to interrupt it?

She really hadn't needed the reminder that she'd be having a better time were it Zach sitting across from her, maybe coming home to help her make dinner. Kissing her again. Backing her down the hallway to her bedroom.

Stop it. And stop staring. She focused on her coffee cup. Out of the corner of her eye, she caught the bemused look Caleb directed at Zach.

Great.

Zach's ill-looking complexion reddened. "Look, I'm sorry for interrupting. You two, uh, have fun."

Fantastic. She'd inadvertently wrecked what should have been a great day for Zach.

And worse, that was not the face of someone only experiencing "a little chemistry."

The next morning Cadie glared at her schedule.

9:00: Zach.

1:00: Zach.

Today, tomorrow, Friday.

Now that he'd been cleared for full-time work and regular exercise, she'd scale him back to fewer appointments for future weeks, leaving three more days of double appointments. She could handle that, right? If she could manage six full weeks of seeing him twice daily, a measly few more days should be child's play.

Her gut wobbled. As if. Not after that kiss, and after he interrupted her coffee date with Caleb.

"Cadie?" Lauren poked her head around Cadie's office door. "You had a shipment come in. Do you want it in the storage area?"

Cadie crossed her arms. "You didn't answer my texts."

Lauren blushed. "My phone was dead."

"Since yesterday afternoon?"

"Well—"

"If you're going to meddle with my life," Cadie spat, "you should at least have the guts to admit it."

"Zach had news." Lauren's voice came out weakly. "He seemed to want to tell you…"

"It could have waited."

Lauren leaned against the door frame and lifted a shoulder as if to say "Too late."

"It was embarrassing, Lauren."

"Meeting a hot guy at Peak Beans was embarrassing? Can't be Mr. Right, then."

"No, he's not." No guy was. "But I wasn't embarrassed by Caleb. More by the fact that Zach had no idea I was on a date and then felt badly for interrupting."

"I don't see you and Caleb caring about a quick interruption, so what's the big deal?"

Oh, just the fact that for a fraction of a second something had crossed Zach's face that Cadie imagined he never wanted out in the world. Nor did she want to know if she was right on that prediction. "It was manipulative."

Lauren's mouth gaped before creasing with resignation. "I know."

Cadie threw up her hands. "So why did you do it?"

"I thought you might need a nudge."

Irritation flared in Cadie's chest. "We're not in nudge territory yet."

"And if you hadn't been talking to Garnet about it, I wouldn't have, but you did, and it's so freaking obvious Zach has feelings for you that I thought—"

"No, Lauren." She pointed at her sister. "You *didn't* think."

Lauren's resignation turned to hurt. "That's harsh."

"Did you ever stop to consider that maybe you're not privy to every conversation that Zach and I have? And that there are dynamics going on that you don't know about?"

Lauren took a seat in the chair up against the wall and sat sideways so she was facing the desk. "I take it there are dynamics?"

"Yep." Cadie popped the "p" sound and swiveled her chair to look at her sister. "He was hurt, Lauren."

"I'm sorry." Sincerity threaded Lauren's apology.

"Me, too."

"So you are interested in him?"

"Yes! Well… Sort of… But it's not going to work. I mean—Sam—and…argh." Cadie rested her forearms on the desk and plunked her forehead on top of them. "Lauren?"

"Yeah?" A painful softness marked the word.

"Have you seen how sweet he is with Ben?"

"This is not about Ben, Cadie."

"Yeah, it is. And about Zach being caring and reliable—"

"And hot as sin," Lauren added.

"Your words."

"Your thoughts."

Cadie groaned. "You're right. I'm full-on attracted to him." Somehow, admitting the thing she'd expected to keep to herself indefinitely was easier while burying her face in her arms. "But I don't want to fall in love right now."

"Hon—"

A gruff, deep-pitched throat cleared in the doorway, cutting off whatever Lauren had been about to say. Cadie went rigid and slowly brought her head up to look Zach in the eye.

He met her stare with pointed seriousness. "I'm sure *Caleb* will be disappointed to hear that."

"Right," she said, her tight throat garbling her attempt to speak. "Caleb."

"Caleb," Lauren echoed, shooting to her feet. "Exactly. I'll, uh, leave you to your appointment."

As her sister left the room, Zach tilted his chin in a silent farewell and fixated on the wall behind Cadie. The book he held in his hand, a functional movement text she'd lent him, made a faint slapping sound as he rapped it against his other palm.

"You know," he rasped, "I'm betting Caleb understands. And probably has his own reasons for agreeing with you that anything more than a coffee date wouldn't be feasible."

She blinked. Wait. Had he overheard enough of the conversation to have clued in that she and Lauren had been talking about him, not Caleb? Was he speaking in code? Or did he truly think she was disappointed that her date had been a flop?

Damn it. She didn't want to have this conversation. But lying, or even making excuses, wasn't going to help. "I'm not interested in Caleb."

The rhythm of the book against his palm sped up. "I know."

"And I was serious about not wanting to fall in love right now."

His green gaze landed on her with a wallop of regret. "I know that, too."

"But I am happy you've been cleared for activity. And I'm going to work the hell out of you to get you ready for Whistler."

"Thank you." He dropped the book on her desk, finality echoing in the thunk of paper against faux-mahogany. "That's all we can do."

The grit lying over his words abraded her insides. Pain shot through her belly. She nodded and led him out of her office into the main PT area. "Priority number one."

Chapter Nine

The myriad last-minute tasks involved with moving gave Cadie a welcome distraction for the remainder of the week. It didn't erase the ache in her heart, but at least it kept her busy enough so her family and friends stayed clueless about her emotional state.

Saturday dawned bright and cloudless, promising another overly warm August day, and by 8:00 a.m. her family had descended. Andrew, Lauren and Tavish set to loading the small U-Haul, and her dad and Mackenzie took Ben out in the backyard to play with his new cousin before the sun chased them into the shade.

Cadie was in the middle of hurriedly wiping down the counter from the breakfast of fruit and bagels they'd all wolfed down when Zach strolled in, work boots thumping on the tile. He wore a rugby jersey with the sleeves cut off to T-shirt length. Holy crap, she wanted to run her fingers along the stripes ringing his broad chest. Grabbing her water bottle from next to the fruit bowl, she took a swig to wet her parched throat. "Morning. Didn't expect to see you before noon."

"Gonna be another scorcher," he said blithely. "Good thing we're getting this done early."

She crossed her arms. He was *not* playing moving man today. "We?"

He straightened. "Lauren told me to come in and grab a bagel, and that most of your stuff is in the spare room."

"Oh, heck no." She grabbed a dish towel from the handle of the stove and flicked it at his stomach. "You are not lifting one box, let alone a room full of them."

He raised a brow. "Pretty sure I'm cleared for some of the lighter stuff now that I'm cane-free."

"It's too risky."

"So's skiing."

"And you're not ready to ski yet."

He gestured through the doorless archway to her siblings, who were turning the air blue as they maneuvered the cedar chest Cadie had inherited from their grandmother down the hall toward the front door. "Your family is helping. You're not treating your pregnant sister like an invalid, so I'd appreciate the same gesture."

"Given the baby's no bigger than a lime, my pregnant sister *isn't* an invalid."

His eyes narrowed. "And I am?"

"Nope, but you were a few months ago, so I'd rather you not return to that state."

Closing his eyes, he tipped his head back, bracing his hands on the back of his neck. "Give me a task, Cadie."

The slump of his shoulders warned her to tread easy on his pride. She gentled her tone. "It can't be moving my crap."

"Something else then. Please."

"Um… Ben and I usually go to a Parent-and-Tot art class on Saturdays, but we were going to skip it today. If you're desperate for something to do, you could take him."

His jaw ticked and he released his grip on his neck. "The class is at the community center?"

"Yeah."

"Have you packed your stroller already?"

She shook her head. "It's in the trunk of my car."

"Okay. I'll walk him over there and take him to art class. Then we can hit up the park and meet you at the apartment for nap time. Unless you want him to sleep here."

And there went her heart again, flipping like a tiny gymnast. The only thing better than the sound of Zach doing all those sweet things with her son would be getting to do them with both of them. "You don't mind? That's a lot of activity."

"All under control," he said. "Anything in particular you want me to pack him for lunch?"

She opened her mouth to give a list of options but snapped it shut again. *He wants to be helpful. So let him be helpful.* Relief flooded her—despite their kiss, he was still her rock. "Whatever's in the fridge—you know what he eats." She swallowed the lump that rose in her throat. "Zach?"

He brushed a strand of hair off her face. "Yeah?"

The truth popped out before she could stop it. "You're the best."

"I can't get him to calm down," Cadie said of her wailing son, all the frustration of a long day—topped off by Ben not settling in—rending her voice. She stood in her son's new room, furnished only with his crib and a change table. If she'd actually allowed Zach to pitch in with loading and unloading boxes this morning, it would have given them time to get more of the unpacking done, but she had continued to stubbornly refuse. And he hadn't pushed. She was at the end of her rope. He could tell she was trying to be soothing, but she was upset to the point of erratic rocking.

He rubbed a hand on his breastbone. Watching her suffer was killing him.

So fix it. He couldn't follow through on his first instinct, to kiss away her distress. But Ben—there, he had skills he could use.

"Here, honey, let me try." Scooping a hand under Ben's bottom, he cupped the back of the baby's head and started a slow rock until Ben's shriek turned to a quieter cry. His blond hair was damp, partly from the bath Cadie had given him but also sweat from his twenty-minute scream-fest.

An unsettling wave crashed over Zach. He would do anything for this kid. He would especially do anything for the kid's mother. Who the hell knew what that would look like months, years, from now? Worries for another day. Tonight he'd help her salvage her sanity. "Shh, kiddo. Give your *mutti* a break." He kissed Ben's head while peeking at Cadie. "Where's Bun-Bun?" Ben was incurably attached to the toy.

Cadie's face crumpled. "I can't find it. It must have gotten stuck in a box somewhere."

Ben's cry reached a crescendo again, likely at Cadie's panicked tone. "He'll live without it for a night, Cadence."

"Ugh, but will I?"

"Yeah, you'll be fine." He rocked Ben a little deeper and switched to Spanish. Speaking a different language sometimes distracted the little guy, so it was worth a try. "Hey, buddy. I know it's been a long day. And this is a new place, and you're not sure about that. But your mommy's exhausted. So are you. Make you a deal—go to sleep without the rabbit and I'll buy you four more for your birthday."

Ben stilled in his arms and lifted his head, blue eyes serious. He let out a whimper.

"Promise. Four bunnies, coming up."

As if the kid understood, he said, "Bu-Bu."

Cadie's mouth turned down at the corners. And with Ben quiet, he heard her stomach growl. She pressed a hand to her abdomen. "Oh, shoot. Dinner. I'll need to order—"

"It's done. Chan's. Why don't you go wait for the delivery guy? We can look through the boxes for the missing lovey after we eat."

"Zach…" Something flickered in her eyes. *Longing? Damn.* Given his instinct was to give Cadie what she wanted, knowing she was feeling anything close to need was too much for him to handle.

Ten minutes later Cadie closed the door behind the delivery guy and set to arranging sweet-and-sour boneless pork and chow mein on the counter. Her kitchen wasn't nearly set up, but she'd managed to get newly purchased plates and glasses in the cupboard. The apartment, as Tavish had explained, was mostly furnished—handy, considering she'd brought very little from Colorado when she'd moved. After the funeral, she'd packed up her clothes, books, art and personal stuff, had filled a box of Sam's most important treasures for her then unborn, unnamed baby, and had invited Sam's friends to help themselves to the rest. Given income was often scarce in ski towns, the condo she'd lived in for her short marriage had been stripped to the walls by sunset.

This apartment she could take the time to make her own. Not having to worry about dining room and living room furniture or a bedroom suite had made it easier to leave her dad's in a short time frame. And once she'd realized she wanted to move, there'd been no need to delay. She'd craved proof she was moving forward.

Letting out a breath, she stared at the three stacks of boxes haphazardly occupying the living room floor. She had the bones of a home here, she just needed to put them together. Once the kitchen and bedrooms were organized—and, let's be honest, priority number one was to find Bun-Bun—she could go about filling the shelving unit in the living room with knickknacks and could hang her family themed gallery wall in the spot in the dining room where Tavish had previously displayed some of his photography.

Turning to the fridge to take out two beers, she chuckled. Ben and Zach's artistic effort from the morning—a vibrant mess of sponge-painted circles and thumb prints arranged to look like *The Very Hungry Caterpillar*—was fastened to the fridge with one of the scattered magnets left behind. Given Tavish had thoroughly emptied the place of his personal effects, the stained-glass magnets might have even belonged to Mackenzie. No matter the source—she was just happy to be able to provide proof of occupancy. The splash of color served as a temporary brightener in the small-but-functional kitchen. And the thought of Zach, Ben on his lap and hands covered in paint? She couldn't not smile at that.

Speaking of Zach and her son, she hadn't heard anything in about five minutes. Her hand hovered over the monitor she'd plugged in next to the single-cup coffeemaker. It bordered on an invasion of privacy to listen in, but curiosity prodded her into flicking the switch.

A low baritone came out of the speaker. She didn't understand it—Zach was singing in Spanish—but she didn't need to. The sound gripped her heart and twisted.

What was she doing with this man, sending him to Ben's art class and dumping bedtime duties on him?

Teasing herself? Teasing him?

Her breathing picked up and her nose pinched. Gripping the counter, she leaned against the cool surface and unsuccessfully tried to breathe away the tears. Fat drops slid off her chin and splashed onto the polished, green-flecked stone.

Why had her sister-in-law picked that color for her counters? Had she wanted Cadie to have to stare at granite the exact shade of Zach's eyes every morning as she fixed Ben's breakfast?

Self-centered much? Tone it down.

Obeying her inner voice, she sucked in a gulp of air and stole a piece of sweet, delicious pork from under the foil lid of the take-out container. Her stomach growled even louder now, but Zach had been kind enough to order her dinner and take over with Ben. She wasn't going to start eating without him.

"Good grief. Why'd you wait?" came his voice from the hallway. "You're starving."

The stress of the day yanked at her composure, unraveling it like the day last week when Ben had crawled into the bathroom and pulled at the toilet paper until half the roll was in shambles on the floor. "You know, there's a fine line between gratitude and rage, Cardenas."

"Huh?"

Another tear trailed down her cheek and she wiped it with the back of her hand. "One of these days, I might actually believe I'm doing this right."

Head cocked to the side, he stopped a few feet away from her. "What are you talking about?"

"You got Ben to sleep. Without that stupid rabbit, no less. It usually takes me a half hour or more to get him

to settle on a night he's *not* freaking out." She snuck another morsel of pork with her fingers and popped it into
her mouth. Self-doubt ground at her confidence.

Zach reached out as if to palm her cheek but dropped
his hand before making contact. He slowly shook his
head. "You're doing this right every day, Cadence."

"But you—"

"It's like opening a mayonnaise jar," he said with a
lopsided grin. "You loosened the lid for me." With a few
quick motions he peeled the covers off the containers and
shoved a pair of chopsticks in her hand. "Eat. Please."

She reached for the cupboard. "My plates are unpacked."

"Plates are overrated." Picking up his own chopsticks
and rubbing them together to get rid of wooden slivers,
he plucked a deep-fried shrimp out of the golden stack
and chewed with relish. Pleasure softened his expression
as he closed his eyes.

"We haven't eaten off a counter in, say, five years,"
she said. The memory of sharing reheated Chinese food
with Sam and Zach—and Zach's girlfriend at the time, to
be fair—after a long day on the slopes emerged from the
ether, making her smile. So many of her thoughts about
Sam were wrapped up in his attitude toward her pregnancy that it was always a nice surprise to have a happy
one float to the surface.

They ate in silence, both leaning against the counter
and shoveling bites into their mouths like it was their
first meal in a week.

Once she finally felt like she had a handle on her
blood sugar, Cadie rested her chopsticks on a take-out
container lid. "How'd your walk feel today? That wasn't
a short distance for you."

"It was walking," he said grumpily.

"I know. But that's further than you've done on the treadmill."

"You didn't say anything at the time."

"No," she said, reining in the instinct to get defensive, "because I knew you'd be okay. But I wanted to ask on the off chance I was wrong."

He crossed his arms on the counter and stared at the lurid red puddle of sauce in one of the aluminum containers, all that remained of the pork. "I'm going to need to push myself if I'm going to be ready to hike the glacier in five weeks."

"There's pushing yourself and there's being stupid."

He quickly fisted and splayed a hand.

"I'm not saying you're going to be stupid—"

"Aren't you?" he murmured.

"Absolutely not. But we have to be just as regimented about your recovery now that you're walking crutches-free. There's still no guarantee you'll be ready to go. Who knows how it's going to feel? You'll have to play it by ear."

"The film will get done. I will be on that mountain," he said from between gritted teeth.

"You know, Sam's not going anywhere. Delaying for the sake of your health…"

He crumpled his napkin into a tight ball and threw it forcefully into the paper bag the food had come in. "I made a promise. I'm following through on it. Period."

Anger balled under her ribs, pushing up, threatening to crack her bones. "Your health is more important than a promise to get a stupid film made, Zach. It's not like Sam was the poster boy for sticking with commitments."

"And I don't want to share his flaws," he said quietly. "I told him I'd do it."

Lacing her fingers behind her spine, she arched her back, trying to loosen the cramps clenching her rib cage.

"You told him that after the avalanche? How could Sam even have been thinking about the film then? Why the hell was it even a remote priority?"

"It's not that simple," Zach said, sounding strained, like he was fighting a cramp of his own.

She opened her eyes to make sure he was okay. Elbows on the counter, strong back slumped, he cradled his head in his hands. His fingers kneaded his scalp.

"Zach…" Placing her hand between his shoulder blades, she rubbed a tentative circle over his shirt. "What's not that simple?"

His fingers stilled, strands of his thick hair sticking out between his knuckles like tufts of wild grass. "My promise, Cadence. Promises."

A flicker of warning teased her spine at his emphasis on the plural. "You want to talk about it?"

"No."

"Should you talk about it?"

"I have." A breath shuddered from his lips. "You're not the only person who's seen a counselor."

"I know. And that's good." But something told her Zach had let go of his survivor's guilt about as well as Cadie had her regret about the state of her marriage before Sam's death. Maybe he'd hidden feelings from his therapist, too. Hadn't felt like seeing disgust on the face of a paid professional.

A dark shadow crossed through Zach's eyes. "After we rescued him he didn't overtly ask me to finish the film. But he did ask me to make sure he wasn't forgotten. And the film is the most effective way for me to follow through on that."

For God's sake, Sam. You weren't happy with solely tying up my life? You had to make Zach beholden to your memory? But the explanation did clear up Zach's determination to get to Whistler. It was more than just finishing up a project or memorializing a friend—Zach wouldn't take a vow like that lightly.

"Hey," she said quietly, wrapping her arms around his hunched body from the side and resting her cheek on his shoulder. His muscles went rigid, but he didn't slough off the embrace. "You're doing your best."

"Am I, Cadie? Was it my best when I kissed you?" Bitter shame dripped from his tone. He turned sideways, making her release her hug, and rested a hand on her hip. "Am I doing my best when I want you every damned day?"

She blinked. Well, that was sharpening a point on what had been a blunt pencil. "I—" She slowly blew air out between flat lips, the sibilant sound riding over, but not covering, his ragged breathing. "I don't think I can answer that for you."

His thumb arced a path on her hip and her breath hitched. "Yeah, let's label that a rhetorical question," he said. "The only person who needs to worry about my promise is me."

"You said *promises*. More than one," she pointed out.

He grunted noncommittally.

Curiosity poked her. What had he and Sam talked about on that mountain that Zach was so reluctant to discuss? She knew full well he'd never divulged the whole story. What he had shared—that Sam loved her and was sorry—hadn't simplified or eased the grieving process any, so she hadn't asked for the rest. Now, though—if she wanted to truly move on, she needed all the information.

She placed a hand on his shoulder and teased the seam of his rugby jersey. It was easier to focus on the burgundy cotton instead of the raw regret ravaging the planes of his face. "What else did he say?"

"After we dug him out?" he croaked, scrubbing the

back of his neck with the knuckles of his free hand. He was still idly rubbing her hip with the other—did he even know he was touching her there?

She wasn't about to forget. A slow burn crackled at her core, each slow stroke of his hand stoking the burgeoning flame.

"Yeah. While they were packing him up for transport." Though Sam had broken his neck when the avalanche swept him off a cliff, he could have survived had he been dug out sooner. He'd been buried with a decent air pocket, so oxygen deprivation hadn't been an issue. But chest trauma had led to shock and he'd gone into cardiac arrest on the helicopter. By the time he'd arrived in Vancouver, it had been too late. And she knew Zach blamed himself for the fifteen minutes it had taken the rescue crew to travel from base camp to the avalanche field. That they had talked about, desperate attempts on her part to help him see he couldn't have changed the outcome.

He'd never budged on that. Maybe he would on this, though. "What did he say, Zach?" she prodded when he stayed silent.

"Like I've told you before—sorry, and I love you."

She let out a frustrated sigh. "That was to me. What did he say to *you*, besides making sure he wasn't forgotten?"

He pressed his fingers into his eyes. "Nothing unusual, Cadence."

She narrowed her eyes. Ever since he broke the dam and had started using her nickname on occasion, she'd gotten the impression that when he had called her Cadence it was with affection. This time, though, he was throwing up a wall.

"Not unusual doesn't mean not important," she said. "Why do you want to know so badly?"

"Because it feels like there are pieces missing in the puzzle, and I'm ready to slot things into place."

Muttering a curse, he scooted between her and the counter. His hips rested on the granite and he tugged her into the V of his long legs. Clammy palms clasped both her hands and he stared at her knuckles as if they held the answers to the origins of the universe.

"It's not—" He hesitated. "I don't want you to take this the wrong way. So know that I think you're capable and resourceful and downright amazing with everything you do."

"Okaaaaay..."

"And regardless of Sam's perspective on what he asked, I've only ever taken it to mean that we function better with support. Everyone does."

"Zach." She lifted one of her hands, still joined with his, and nudged him under the chin until he looked at her. "What did he ask?"

An odd mix of guilt and resignation crossed his face. "He wanted me to take care of you."

Defensiveness rose but she took a calming breath. Nothing odd about Sam wanting her looked after—really, it was a heartening thing to know he'd been concerned about her welfare, given the last time they'd spoken they'd thrown around words like "separation" and "divorce." But for Zach... Sam's request clarified his behavior. Fleshed out his move to Sutter Creek. "I figured you followed me here because you felt guilty."

He lifted a shoulder. "Column A, column B."

"I see." What a load of new information—she didn't know where to begin to file it away.

"You're not pissed?"

"That you and he both cared—*care*—enough to want to make sure I'm okay? It's somewhat comforting, to be honest. He and I left things in such an ugly place…" And she felt all the worse for the number of times her inner shadows suggested she might be better off without Sam. A sob crept out, echoing in the tiny, galley kitchen.

"Shh. It's okay." He lifted one of her hands to his mouth and pressed a kiss to her knuckles. A shimmer of pleasure warmed her skin.

"I hope so." Her voice hitched from the echo of his lips on her hand. "Like I said the other day, I do need to hang my own shingle now."

He squeezed her fingers. "You can do it."

"I haven't so far. I couldn't have made it through pregnancy or Ben's first year alone."

"I was happy to do it. I really do love living here, working here. It was a nice place to land. It would have been too hard to stay in Colorado."

"Do you think…do you think he would have supported me?" Her voice cracked. "I've never been able to believe he would have."

One gentle tug from Zach's hand and she was up against his broad chest, wrapped in his arms. The bands of muscle held her up and she ringed her arms around his ribs, pressed her cheek next to the quarter placket of buttons on his shirt, and let her knees sag. She breathed out the guilt until she stopped the tears from coming.

"His specific words were to 'take care of Cadie and the baby.' I can only assume he meant in his stead."

"I wish I had your optimism."

"Thinking otherwise feels like a betrayal. Hard to ask for your friend to clarify when he's effing dead."

"Something I've mulled over a hell of a lot myself."

"Cadie…" The stark fear in his eyes grabbed at her insides. "I promise, I'm not trying to take his place."

"Didn't think you were," she said.

Every time you hold my son, I imagine you in it, though.

"I can't do that to him—"

"I didn't think you were," she repeated.

A breath shuddered from his lungs. "Every time I've wanted you, though—*every time*—I've had to deal with the reality that I've gotten dangerously close to trying just that."

"Zach—"

"I *have*. I've pictured it—"

"Zach." The self-loathing darkening his green eyes to a bottomless crevasse—it was too hard to see him like this.

"What kind of friend would—"

"Stop. You've been nothing but loyal." And he deserved to be free. Deserved to know that whatever existed between them, however temporary the physical attraction might be, didn't make him a bad friend to Sam.

"A loyal friend doesn't move in on his buddy's wife, Cadence."

"And you haven't." She rested her palm against his cheek, stroking her thumb along the evening stubble. "We're not getting involved with each other. So we kissed. And—correct me if I'm wrong—you want to do it again. Well, I do, too."

"Again."

Always. Keeping in the full truth, she jerked a nod.

He dropped his forehead to hers. His rapid breaths warmed her skin. "Why?"

A bark of laughter escaped her throat. "Because you're eighteen levels of sexy? And I haven't been intimate with anyone in over a year and a half? And just for one night it would be nice to feel like a desirable woman again?"

He swore again, an exclamation this time instead of a complaint.

"Well, that's one word for it."

"Cadence…"

"Yeah?"

"You're miles above 'desirable,'" he growled. "But is acting on that something we can live with?"

"Is there that much of a difference between knowing how we feel and acting on how we feel?"

His pupils widened. "I want to answer no."

"So answer no."

Brows drawn in confusion, he tightened his arms around her. "No? Or yes? And to your question, or to this?" His thumb kissed her lips with a tenderness she'd only imagined.

The buzz of the refrigerator matched the hum of adrenaline in her chest. She reached for his shirt and gripped two handfuls of the thick cotton. "I'm not looking for anything permanent, Zach." *But I do want you. All of you.*

She couldn't admit that, could she? The smells of warm summer and his minty shampoo swirled around her. Need rose from her belly through her chest. She pressed into his hard muscles, itching to get closer. All around and inside, and…she shut her eyes, her brain blistering with the image of losing all barriers between her hands and his skin and taking him into her body. She rose on her toes, heat pooling at the apex of her thighs. Her nipples tightened as the lacy material of her half camisole dragged, caught between her sensitive flesh and the wall of his chest.

For the love of… Just say it. "I do want you. Just for tonight."

He groaned. "Ah, honey. Are you serious?"

"Very." Her eyes were level with his neck. A tantalizing hollow of sun-kissed skin begged for her tongue. Lowering her mouth to his collarbone, she brushed her lips—first closed, then open—across the divot.

He shivered in her embrace and his Adam's apple bobbed. "I don't know."

"Yeah, I'm getting that." Sighing, she dropped back on her heels and tried to step away.

"No, wait." One hand pressed high by her shoulder blade, the other low by the waistband of her leggings, preventing her escape. He was so tense she could almost count ten distinct fingertip impressions in her skin.

"I do know," he continued. "I'm just…"

Scared. His voice vibrated with it.

Well, for one night, she could be fearless for both of them. A bolt of courage ripped through her muscles and she dug her fingers into his thick hair. Pulling his mouth to hers, she finally tasted him. Fortune cookies and masculine spice. Perfection.

She nipped his lower lip. "You're 'just' going to follow me to my room. And then make good on every hot look you've laid on me this past month."

This past month.

That was significant somehow. *How?*

Who cares? Go away, brain. Only the skill of his lips moving against her mouth mattered, the fingertips of his hand as they pushed the back of her tank top up and snuck under her waistband. She squirmed as his fingers teased the skin along the base of her spine. "Have sex with me, Zach. And tomorrow we'll forget it ever happened."

Chapter Ten

Forget the inevitable bliss of Cadie's heels hooked around Zach's waist and heaven pressed against his hardening shaft?

Impossible.

But lose his chance to have her naked body under his over something as trivial as a memory that would haunt him for the rest of his cursed existence?

No damned way.

He let her take his hand and guide her to her room, his determination building with each step. They weren't forging a relationship. She didn't want one; he couldn't have one and keep his promise. But a single night where she could take the edge off—that qualified as helping her, really. And he wanted her too much to poke more holes into that Swiss cheese logic.

His palms cupped the perfect curve of her ass, fixing her to his aching front. Her mouth devoured his and his tongue flooded with sweetness and sex and something alluringly Cadie. And then his knees knocked into her bed and she squirmed against him, simultaneously scrambling to get his shirt off while pulling him on top of her on the bare mattress. The room, with unpacked suitcases stacked next to an oversize armchair and boxes piled on the still empty dresser, left a lot to be desired for ambience, but who cared? He had Cadence, and she was pressing a line of frantic kisses to one of his naked pecs while peeling off her tank top.

He gently ringed his thumbs and forefingers around her wrists before she could lift the garment over her torso. "My job, honey."

She fell back on her elbows and stared at him, pupils dilated and lower lip caught between her teeth. The picture of feminine sensuality. A rumble of approval broke in his chest as he knelt in front of her, her slim legs draped, one on each side, over his spread knees. He stroked his hands along the tops of her legging-covered thighs. *Oh, yeah.* He could lean down and bury his face between her thighs in two seconds if he wanted to. But he was only going to get one night to enjoy all the delights wrapped up in Cadie. He planned to savor each torturous, pleasure-soaked second.

Planned to make sure she did the same.

"What do you like, *belleza*?" he asked, still running his hands in a slow pattern on her legs. He was hard as an effing chairlift tower, straining against his boxers and ripstop shorts.

"Being naked," she complained with a grin.

"Yeah?" Pale skin peeked from between the gathered edge of her tank and the low-slung waist of her yoga capris, making his mouth water. He drew a meandering line through the sweet, bare strip. "Like this skin here?"

She gasped. "Mmm, more of that, yes."

Rising up on his knees, he snagged the edge of her tank with both his pointer fingers. He pushed, the slow ascension of fabric exposing a creamy plane of stomach. His tongue wanted in on this, badly. He pressed his lips to her navel. Once, twice, then licked a path up to where he'd paused removing her shirt, right in the notch of her rib cage.

"Slowpoke." She tore off the slip of fabric and tossed it aside.

"Thought I said that was my job." He tried to put a playful, gruff edge on the words but the sight of her breasts cupped by her bra, the pebbled shadows of her rose nipples visible through sheer, pale pink lace, turned his voice to a croak.

"You don't seem disappointed with the results." She reached for her messy topknot and pulled out the elastic, freeing the tumble of dark, silken curls. They fell in sexy, chaotic waves around her shoulders. Holy mother. Now that he'd seen her hair like this, it was going to be hard not to coax her into wearing it down every time he saw her.

"You're gorgeous." He ran his tongue along his lips and pressed another kiss to her rib cage below the edge of her delicate lingerie. With a gentle finger, he circled the lower curve of one of her breasts. She dug her fingers into his hair and squirmed. Her legs were still draped haphazardly around his hips, her impatient movements teasing her center against the bottom of his erection.

He hummed his pleasure against her skin. Cupping her breast with his palm, he mouthed her peaked nipple and lightly scraped his teeth along the wet fabric, eliciting a moan. Her fingers tightened, pulling at his scalp, and he flexed his hips. His shorts were thin enough that heat sank through, blistering his ability to think. Grinding against Cadence's sex was a religion unto itself. Something to be worshipped. Something he could devote himself to with fanatical fervor.

"That—" she gasped "—is exactly what's been missing from my life."

"Me, too." He tipped his pelvis forward again and wasted no time in sliding her out of her bra and bottoms. Wow. Nothing like having a naked, stunning woman reclining in front of a guy to make his fingers stutter while trying to undo the button on his shorts. A tousled halo of curls framed her face and the more he struggled with his clothes, the wider her smile grew.

"Let me," she offered. She knelt in front of him, nudging his shoulders, forcing him to spin and fall backward onto the mattress. A swift motion or two and his shorts were on the floor, followed by his boxers.

She took his length in a firm grip, stroked, and his eyes rolled back in his head. He moaned his ecstasy and muttered a curse.

"This'll be even better," she promised. Straddling him, she settled her wet, aroused flesh over his aching sex and rocked. Her palms and fingers gripped his shoulders as she rode him, cradling his erection between her thighs.

"I—ah… That's—" The slim fraction of his brain still able to form words gave up. He reached for her face and drew her down, kissing her in a tangle of lips and half-formed phrases. Who knew what the hell language he was speaking? Didn't matter. She moved with him, her hands dancing along his body, ratcheting his arousal to the breaking point.

Breaking. Damn. "Cadie, do you have a condom handy?"

She sat up straight, her hands falling to her sides. "I—

Crap. Where are—? Yes. I think I know the box I shoved them in."

Empty dissatisfaction hollowed his belly as she bolted from the room. But she was back in a minute, tearing open the package and sheathing him with nimble fingers.

Doubt stole some of the arousal from her face. She tugged at her bottom lip with her teeth and stretched out beside him, curving against his side. "Zach?"

His stomach filled with dread. "You want to stop?"

She laughed. "Are you kidding me?"

"No," he said, confused. "Not at all. You looked unhappy and unless you're one hundred percent on board..."

Resting her head on his shoulder, she took his hand and pressed it to the slight curve of her belly, sliding it down into the tidy thatch of curls between her thighs. "Does that feel unhappy to you?"

"Can't say it does." It felt like the happiest place on earth to him.

He slicked a finger between her folds. Her arousal coated his fingers and he swirled the nub in a way he knew would bring her pleasure.

Back arching, she whimpered.

"I want you, Zach."

He could get way too used to hearing that declaration on her lips. "I had to be sure. Didn't like seeing you with anything less than a smile on your face." But he sure loved the expression she wore now. Lust-soaked and flushed, she looked like she wanted more than his fingers touching her between her legs.

"I was feeling a little silly," she breathed. "I liked being on top, but I really, well, I wanted this." Pulling at his waist, she rolled him into the cradle of her hips. His arousal nestled against hers. *Holy... Control yourself,*

Cardenas. Bracing his elbows on either side of her shoulders, he smoothed a hand down her cheek and kissed her with the reverence she deserved. He thrust, senses reeling with the scent of cherries and the clasp of her tight, slick passage and every inch of her sweet skin, so soft against his own.

The movement of sex, of Zach's body lighting every one of Cadie's nerve endings on fire, was slow, an agonizing pace she sensed he'd set purely to torture her. She clung to his shoulders as their hips moved in a synchronism she'd have expected had they been together for a year, not for a few frantic minutes. And with each of his long, tantalizing strokes, tension built at her core, a desperate clawing toward release.

"We should slow down," she gasped. "Or this'll be done too soon."

"Mmm, I like the idea of you being done. That way you get your pleasure more than once."

"More?"

"As many times as you want." He nibbled and licked along the side of her neck. She tilted her chin, exposing more for him, and he murmured his approval. Shivers danced on her skin from the scrape of his stubble and heated tickle of his breath.

"The giving type, are you?" The antithesis of surprise. He'd been giving almost all of himself to her for a long time. And tonight—all of himself. Every hard inch. His talented hands, too. She slid her hands down his obliques, savoring the strong ropes of muscle under his hot skin.

"You name it, it's yours."

She tightened her thighs around his hips, lining the bundle of nerves aching for more, deeper, now with the delicious friction of his pelvis. "Zach—I just want you…"

...for more than tonight.

She kissed him fiercely, trying to shut her brain off. She had a hot man pressed against her, driving slow waves of pleasure through her body. *Not the time to start dreaming of more.*

"You've got me," he finally replied, lips brushing hers as he mumbled the sweet, devastating promise.

"Just for tonight."

"Yeah." His hand drifted down between their bodies and he toyed with her. Her hips lifted to his hand, needy and seeking the promise of his fingers. The slick slide of his length echoed the rhythm of his hand. He wasn't just touching her. He was consuming her. And she couldn't do anything but arch against him and break apart. White flashed behind her eyes. A cascade of heat consumed her body and tore a moan from her throat, followed by a bolt of fear. Now that he'd touched her soul, there was no way to put herself back together again.

Sometime later, a hazy space marked by frenetic kisses and languid touches alike, Cadie lay with a leg and an arm draped over Zach's body. A few last precious minutes of having full access to every naked part of him. With a finger, she doodled an abstract squiggle in his tidy sprinkling of dark abdominal hair. Her heart raced, every beat reminding her that "just for tonight" was ticking away.

"We didn't do anything wrong, Cadence." His worried tone suggested otherwise.

"Sounds like you need to convince yourself of that as much as you do me."

A gruff protest rumbled from his chest.

"Our reasons were sound, Zach." *I don't regret this.* Ugh, why couldn't she get the words out? *Just say it.*

Because she didn't. Not in the way she'd thought. Guilt over Sam was the last thing on her mind.

He exhaled, a long, telling breath. "I should probably get going."

She nodded.

"Do you need help unpacking tomorrow? Or will I see you for my appointment Monday morning?"

Her body went rigid. *Monday morning? Son of a—* She sprang away, scrambling for her shirt and holding it in front of her body. "Monday! Your *appointment.*"

Confusion crinkled his forehead as he sat and reached for her knee. "What about it?"

"We've talked about the rules before. Not that I'm blaming this on anyone but myself," she said quickly. "I could slough off a kiss, but this was the *definition* of a sexual relationship…"

The pinnacle, really—good God, it had been spectacular. She mentally slapped herself. It was not time for musing on the last hour. Brilliant or not, it was a giant no-no, a massive breach of her code of ethics. Her lower lip started to wobble and she sucked it behind her teeth to stop it from betraying the extent of her worry.

"Hey, now," he soothed, stroking her knee as if she were a panicking child. "It won't be an issue. We agreed to only once, so it's not exactly a relationship. And no one will know but us—"

"*I'll* know." How had she let this happen? He was her client. Why had she not thought of—? Oh, *crap.* She *had.* She'd just ignored the vague warning that there was more at stake than their personal feelings. Had jumped him like a crazed chimpanzee. *Damn. Damn times a thousand.*

"Given we agreed to forget this ever happened," he said, "I don't see—"

"Forgetting was possible when it was just about our

friendship." *Liar. You'll never forget this.* Ignoring the obvious truth, she swallowed the lump in her throat and continued. "But I can't forget when it comes to work."

He withdrew his hand from her knee. Caution laced his voice when he asked, "What are you saying?"

"I can't be your therapist now!" Jumping from the bed, unable to look at his perplexed head tilt for another second, she yanked on her tank and panties and stared out the wide window to the base quad chair in the distance. *I am such an idiot.* She crossed her arms to try to quell the burning shame searing her chest. She'd slept with her client and the wrongness of that had barely crossed her mind. Yeah, he was a hell of a lot more to her than just her client, and she'd been mainly focused on the tangle of their history, on trying not to think about exactly how much more he meant to her. But she still should have clued in to the ethical quandary before she'd ripped his freaking shirt off.

She heard the snick of a zipper and the padding of bare feet across the hardwood floor of her new, now well-christened bedroom.

His hands landed on her shoulders and he squeezed. "*Belleza*, we'll talk about this tomorrow, okay? It'll be all right."

"No, it won't." Especially if he kept calling her by that panty-melting endearment. Her insides went downright gooey at the pretty inflection he put on the syllables. He had to stop that. They had to stop *everything*. Oh Lord, did she have to turn herself in or something? Admit her screw-up to the state licensing board? She'd need to transfer his care to another therapist, at minimum, and that would mean questions. Her eyes stung at the corners and she rubbed at them with the heel of her hand.

"I don't want to leave you like this." His fingers tightened on her essentially bare shoulders.

"You have to leave me like this." *Because I can't handle your hands on me for another second and if I'm not careful I'll throw away my job by begging you to stay...* She jerked out of his grip. "You should have left hours ago. Sleeping over wasn't part of the deal."

His sigh filled the otherwise silent room. "I'll let myself out. And I'll call you in the morning."

Chapter Eleven

Zach lumbered into the physio waiting room early Monday morning, a cranky cloud hovering over him like it had since yesterday. *Try again, Cardenas. You* wish *this was just crankiness.* Dread, more like. Nothing like having his phone calls and texts go unanswered, driving home his colossal mistake.

We'll forget it happened, my ass.

"Zach…" Winnie, the physiotherapy receptionist, studied him with serious brown eyes. "Uh, you're in with Deon this morning."

His stomach crawled. He flattened his lips. Probably gave away his surprise, but it was that or yell something entirely inappropriate in Cadie's workplace. "That's what's in the schedule?"

She nodded. "I didn't change it, so I'm not sure why. Maybe it's an error."

"It's not. Cadence must have changed it." A fist clamped around his heart. "She here?"

Winnie shook her head. "All her morning appointments have been rescheduled. Maybe she needed extra time to unpack her new place?"

"Must have," he lied. Extra time to avoid him was more like it. He muttered a choice piece of profanity, one he'd learned from his cousins on his first visit to Bavaria as a preteen. There really was nothing like the guttural brevity of German when a person needed a solid oath. But words failed to relieve the pressure behind his ribs.

"Cardenas!" Deon Wilson poked his shaved head around the glass partition and crooked a dark brown finger. "Less gabbing, more rehabbing."

Zach forced a groan at the cheesy rhyme, knowing the therapist would expect it. They ran in the same search and rescue circles and had developed an amiable relationship since Zach had moved to town, occasionally snowboarding together or sharing a Friday beer at a pub gathering. Zach appreciated the guy's easygoing nature. Would have been eager to work with him but for the utter cock-up motivating Cadie's abandonment. No matter. He wasn't dragging Deon into his drama. "They teach you that cutesy crap in your training?"

"Client Amusement 101."

He walked over to the other man, hopefully out of Winnie's earshot. "Look, I don't know what Cadence told you, but—"

"She told me if you didn't stick around for the appointment, she'd recommend your doctor put you back on crutches." From the uncertainty in Deon's gaze, he couldn't decide if Cadie was serious or not. "You two have a falling out? When she called me yesterday to switch things around, she implied you knew about the change."

"Something like that," Zach mumbled. He itched to ditch his session and find her before his shift started at work. But if she was barking about contacting his doctor, he didn't want to test out the threat.

An hour later Deon sent him to the gym to finish on the recumbent bike. A few minutes into the pre-programmed cool-down, Caleb Matsuda sauntered over. Sweat dripped from his brown-black hair and he inventoried Zach with assessing eyes.

"You still limping like you were last week?" the physician asked, stopping in front of the bike and bracing his hands on the display. "I meant to call you and talk to you about that, make sure your doctor didn't jump the gun by letting you walk without a mobility aid."

Zach cocked a brow. "Gotta say, man, I have enough medical professionals on my ass."

Caleb nodded in concession. "Fair."

"Don't worry—I'll be ready to tear up the slopes with you come opening day."

Paling under his tawny olive complexion, Caleb rubbed a hand down his face. "No need to rush on that."

A protest leaped on Zach's tongue but he held it back. He wasn't sure which of them Caleb was referring to when it came to rushing back onto the hill. He hadn't even considered that Caleb might not have been up a mountain since the avalanche. The guy had been a wild man on skis, but if anything could cure an adrenaline addiction, it was getting sucked under a churning wave of snow.

Not to mention discovering three of their friends hadn't been rescued in time.

Zach shook his head, still questioning why he'd been rewarded for making excuses and begging off the morning's filming that day. And again on Hammond's Chute— things could have gone just as sideways with his ski accident. Really, rehab was a small price to pay. Over the course of his freestyle career he'd never missed more than a few weeks due to injury. The reality of six ski-free months struck fear into his hopefully well-healed bones. He'd train until he fell over to avoid looking like an idiot the first time he strapped on skis.

"Did, uh—how'd Cadie's move go?" Caleb inquired.

"Well. I think she'll be happy in her new place." Zach took a swig of water from the bottle he'd stashed in the cup holder. "I wasn't able to help her much. No lifting and all that."

"I'm sure you figured out a way to make yourself useful."

Coughing, he sprayed water across his knees. Yeah, he'd been useful. Three times, to be exact. "Um, we... well..."

Way to be articulate.

The corner of Caleb's mouth played up. "Something else I've been meaning to talk to you about—that date I went on with Cadie—"

"None of my business." Frustration burned through Zach's body and he pushed harder against the pedals.

"You sure about that?"

"Damn sure." One night together, no matter how perfect, didn't give him the right to care if she started seeing someone else. He *should* want her to start seeing someone else. He certainly couldn't be that something more for her. Not if he expected to keep his promises to Sam. And even if he could break them and still live with himself, Cadie shouldn't have to. After how Sam had treated her, she deserved a man above reproach in the reliability department.

"Well, for what it's worth, we won't be going out again. She said she wasn't ready." Caleb cleared his throat. "But then I saw the way she looked at you… Made me wonder if she was telling the truth."

Refusing to entertain the flicker of hope teasing his gut, Zach grabbed his workout towel and wiped the sweat from the back of his neck. "She was."

Caleb crossed his arms. "You want her. Are you freaked out over Sam or something?"

"I came for physio, Matsy, not for talk-about-my-feelings hour."

Inclining his head, the other man drummed the electronic bike display in a nervous pattern and shifted on his feet. "You know, twenty minutes under the snow was plenty of time for me to think about life, to realize it's better to spend it on things that truly matter. And with people I love."

Zach had the "things that truly matter" part down, but spending life with the people he loved… That was trickier. "Can't argue with that."

With a flick of his gaze at Zach's rapidly spinning feet, Caleb raised a brow. "You got something against that machine?"

Zach laced his fingers behind his head and barked out a laugh.

His friend's expression sobered. "I overheard some of what went down between you and Sam the night before the slide, and I'm guessing that's not easy to live with, but Zach, man—focus on the living, not the dead. That's what matters. Every time."

Zach's mouth hung open a fraction. How the hell was he supposed to respond to that?

Leaning in, Caleb clapped Zach on the shoulder, saving him from having to stutter a reply. "Meet you for beers before you go to Whistler?"

"Yeah," Zach said. "You definitely not coming, then?"

"Nah, I'm good leaving that behind me." Caleb strolled toward the exit, leaving Zach to mull over the other man's words.

For one, the guy was full of it. If he wasn't mentally able to get on skis, he was in no way leaving the avalanche behind him. And Zach had a feeling that facing the specter would probably help Caleb out.

But truth had dwelt among the lies. *Focus on the living...* Zach would love to do that, to fall into Cadie and never come up for air. Spinning the pedals, he rubbed his chest, right over his aching heart. Yeah, Sam mattered.

But Cadie and Ben mattered more.

He wasn't going to resist when it came to no longer working with her—she'd drawn her line in the sand. He'd make do with Deon. But if she tried to withdraw from their friendship and from being a father figure for Ben, he'd have to fight. And if he could figure out a way to keep his promises to Sam while exploring something deeper than friendship with Cadie, well—it was a possibility worth contemplating.

As Cadie entered her office Thursday morning, she was willing to crown herself Sutter Creek's Champion Disappearing Act. Avoiding Zach's early appointments? She scheduled her pool-therapy sessions for first thing in the morning. Dodging him in town? She used unpacking as an excuse to stay in after work. Ducking him while he was on shift at the lodge? She didn't visit Andrew at work for any reason.

She'd admit the ghosting routine was less than ideal. But what else was she supposed to do? She didn't know what to say to him. A memory rose from the ether: the second day of ethics class when her professor had eyed the students and lectured, "I shouldn't have to tell you this, but *don't* have *sex* with your *clients*!"

She cringed. *Way to be the lowest common denominator.*

Half of her, though, was glad she could tie her distress to the violation of her ethical code. Meant she didn't have to look too closely at the root of the misery threatening to explode from her every pore, which had nothing to do with her physical therapist's regulations. Far safer to blame it on work and to keep avoiding Zach until she decided what to tell him.

He'd left numerous messages. Voice mails. Texts. A handwritten Post-it for her to call him stuck to her desk Monday morning. Seven letters in impeccable cursive.

Call me.
Z.

Her fingers hadn't worked when she'd tried to throw the note away, so she'd just moved it to the bottom of her computer monitor.

Tuesday he'd stuck it to the screen.

Wednesday to her framed picture of Ben.

It was the most futile Easter egg hunt in the world. But that didn't stop her from sitting in her ergonomic chair and scanning her office today, searching for a square of turquoise paper. Nowhere on her desk or the small supply cabinet… A flash of blue-green caught her eye in the otherwise empty, small recycling bin by the door.

Sadness, inversely proportional in size to the tiny, tight ball resting in the bottom of the bin, walloped her.

He gave up?

She pressed a hand to her throbbing stomach. *It's better this way.* All she had left were her career and her family—

and sleeping with Zach over the weekend had threatened her career *and* the reputation of the family business.

Tears pricked her eyes over her stupidity, but she managed to keep them at bay through her morning appointments. At lunch, she changed out of her running shoes into flip-flops, grabbed her purse and headed for the back door, needing to pick up a few things for Ben's birthday party this Saturday. Her dad was hosting the festivities in his backyard. She'd taken care of the grocery shopping yesterday—driving the forty-five minutes into Bozeman to ensure she didn't run into Zach at the local supermarket—so decorations ranked highest on her short to-do list.

"Cadie!"

Groaning at how close she'd been to escaping unnoticed, she stared at the ceiling as she turned toward her sister. "What?" she snapped.

"Whoa!" Lauren held up her hands. "You have been in a seriously pissy mood all week. Want to fill me in?"

The thought of telling Lauren what happened Saturday night was so absurd, Cadie almost laughed. "Sorry. Didn't mean to bite your head off. I'll be fine once it's the weekend. I just want to get through Ben's birthday—"

"Oh, yeah," Lauren interrupted. "Because children's parties are the definition of calm and regenerating."

"It's not that, it's—" She coughed, didn't bother finishing. Come party time, her ability to dodge Zach would evaporate. But she couldn't un-invite the birthday boy's godfather. Not when he loved Ben so much.

Not when she lo—

No. Don't even think it. He doesn't want that from me. And I'm not free to give it.

"Cadie? I could be off base here, but are you anxious

about celebrating Ben's birthday without Sam?" Lauren ventured.

Cadie's cheeks tingled as the blood drained away. Should she have been thinking about that? For heaven's sake. She really didn't know what she was doing when it came to grieving. Small crap, like opening a magazine to a two-page advertisement for ski boots, made her want to escape to a corner and weep. But she was planning a first birthday party for her son and she hadn't even thought of her son's father.

Mainly because she'd been too busy sleeping with Sam's best friend to spare a thought for Sam. She winced.

Concern wobbled on her sister's face. "Should I not have said that? I never know. Not saying anything, I feel like I'm ignoring an important part of you. Saying something, I feel like I'm jabbing a stick into an abscess—"

"Ew. You're not practicing medicine anymore. Leave the revolting similes behind."

Lauren made a face. "Fine. I meant I feel like I'm making it worse. Either way, I'm making it worse."

"You're not." The only person making Cadie's life worse was Cadie herself.

"You say that. But…"

"I mean it."

Reaching out—up, really, given Cadie had half a foot on her sister—Lauren wrapped her arms around Cadie. "Let me get my wallet and I'll come help you with errands. Do not tell me no. It's my nephew's birthday and I want to buy the balloons and help you hang the streamers."

"I—I wasn't going to say no." Cadie squeezed back. "And thank you for asking about Sam. I'd rather face the painful parts rather than sweep everything under a rug."

Liar. The spike of reality drove into her lungs, stealing her breath. *If that were true, I'd have talked to Zach days ago.*

Late Saturday morning Cadie's dad's backyard brimmed with people—her immediate family and various cousins with small children, plus a couple of parents with kids from Ben's community center class.

Cadie and Lauren had converged on the house for an early breakfast. Then, with their father's help, they had festooned the backyard with the three balloon bouquets acquired by Lauren as well as the requisite streamers and dangling Elmo and Cookie Monster cardboard cutouts they'd found on their lunch hour shopping blitz. The only part of the whole affair holding the birthday boy's attention was the talking helium balloon Lauren had splurged on. Ben sat on his great-great-grandmother's quilt on the grass, repeatedly yanking the balloon's anchor ribbon and setting off the tinny recording.

Elmo loves you. Elmo loves you. Elmo loves you.

Ah, well. The smile on his face and his laughs as he entertained her dad and her aunt made the repetition worth it.

Wanting to make sure everyone was occupied either with a task or with celebrating, Cadie scanned the yard from her perch on the stone patio that curved out from the kitchen sliding door and scanned the backyard. She'd conscripted her siblings for odd jobs. Smoke rose from the barbecue, where Lauren and Tavish snuggled together as they flipped burgers and turned wieners. Shouts of glee tinkled from Andrew's domain on the corner of the lawn. He was waving his arms dramatically, refereeing a fight-to-the-death cornhole match between their aunt's school-age grandkids. And everyone was taking a turn giving Mackenzie a break by snuggling the newest Dawson addition. Cadie would have to go steal her nephew away for a few minutes soon. A month or so from now, they'd wake up and find that Teddy wasn't a newborn anymore. He'd been born early so he was still small, but that wouldn't last forever.

Neither will Ben's little years.

Her eyes stung. How was he one already?

Flip-flop footsteps clapped on the flagstones behind her. She didn't need to turn to know who it was. Only one person was unaccounted for.

"Man, honey." Zach's low tones rumbled through her body as he sidled up to her, carrying an oversize box wrapped in cheerful, dotted paper. "Where did a year go?"

Figured he'd read her mind. She lifted a shoulder at his question and studied him out of the corner of her eye. He wore a short-sleeved, jade-and-brown-plaid, button-down shirt that brought out the green in his eyes. Khaki shorts encased his strong thighs. A flicker of pain glinted in his eyes and the present shifted in his hands, forcing him to juggle and let out a, "Whoops."

No need to overanalyze the source of his discomfort. It wasn't his injuries today. The blame lay entirely with her and her impulsive decision to give in to her physical craving for him. And now look at them—she'd screwed up their personal relationship as well as the professional one. But her son's birthday party wasn't the place to slice open that vein of conversation.

He tilted his head toward the outdoor speaker mounted to a post at the edge of the patio, currently playing Mumford & Sons. "Nice of you not to subject us to Raffi."

"Who?"

Adjusting the present into one arm, he put a hand to his chest in mock outrage. "Did you just ask me who Raffi is?"

"Uh, yeah?"

"The Canadian children's *troubadour*?"

"Key word there, Cardenas—Canadian."

He shook his head, sun glinting off the rich mix of browns that always became more apparent as the summer went on and the sun lightened his hair. "You are missing out. Ben, too. My next day off, I'm making him a Spotify playlist and educating him on 'Baby Beluga.' You've let me waste months of being off work when I could have been building his Raffi repertoire."

"Thank God he's only gone a year without." She smiled in amusement, appreciating he was opening with something inane instead of "So about those naked hours we spent together…" She held out her hands as he shifted the present again. "I can put that on the table for you."

A corner of his full, sexy lips lifted. "I've got it."

He ambled over to the card table she'd designated for presents and, after looking at the small, overflowing surface, placed the box on the ground.

"If nothing else, he'll get a kick out of the ribbon on top and being able to crawl in and out of that box," she said, forcing some semblance of neutral conversation past her constricted throat muscles. With his arms free, she wanted to crawl into them, to hide from the reality of how nothing was the same anymore.

Her heart thrummed a frantic rhythm. She couldn't look at him. But when she shifted her gaze to the yard, all she could see was her sister laughing with Tavish by the barbecue, his hand nestled protectively on her just-rounding stomach. And Andrew and Mackenzie, heads together as they snuggled with Teddy, whispered and grinned and were just generally being adorable. Her neck grew hot and she clenched her teeth. She hadn't been able to share pregnancy and the craziness of the newborn months with a guy who cared and loved their baby and—

She had shared her pregnancy. She had shared the craziness. But she'd done it with a man who could never be hers. With a baby who'd never be theirs. *Their baby...* The wonder of those words.

Words she needed to forget. *Stupid, stupid, stupid.*

She tried to picture Sam singing to a screaming Ben, but the image refused to materialize.

Zach jammed his hands into his pockets. Worry darkened his face as his eyes traveled from the hand she was holding to her stomach to her gaze, so obviously focused on him—

She ripped her palm away from her abdomen. "Cake," she choked out, fleeing for the sliding door and dashing through the open-plan kitchen and into the large pantry.

The room was cool despite the late summer heat. A cold sweat broke out on her brow and neck. She shivered and gripped the edge of the small deep-freeze.

The unmistakable dragging sound of a sliding door drowned out the hum of the freezer, followed by footsteps. Long, even strides she'd memorized this past month. Zach's.

His frame filled the pantry doorway. "What's wrong?"

"Nothing. I need to take the ice-cream cake out of the freezer to soften."

Entering the no-longer-spacious-feeling room, he closed the pocket door behind him and palmed the skin between her shoulder blades, which was bare above the bodice of her favorite summer dress, a thin, cotton number dotted with a tiny red-apple print. She shivered again.

"Hey," he said, voice low and ragged with emotion. "You cold?"

She shook her head, but he ignored her denial and seamed himself to her back. Rubbing his big hands up and down the goose-bump-covered skin of her tense arms, he bent his head to her ear. "You know, with Teddy just being born and Lauren being pregnant, it would be odd if you *didn't* have some emotions to process." He cleared his throat. The hum from his chest buzzed against the skin of her back. "You didn't exactly have an average pregnancy and first year of parenting."

"Well aware," she whispered. "But thanks for the validation."

And for the love of everything holy, Zach, do not figure out it was my inability to share a pregnancy with you, *not what I lost with Sam, that upset me today.*

She tipped her head back. The small motion was all she needed to rest her head in the crook of his neck. Tilting her face to his chin, she savored the rough rasp of his stubble against her forehead. She should have been worried whether someone had noticed him following her inside. That possibility didn't give her the discipline necessary to peel herself away from his caress, though. His hands stilled on her arms. His lips teased the edge of her hairline.

"You have your hair up," he murmured. "I don't think I spent enough time the other night telling you how damned much I loved seeing it around your shoulders." He trailed two fingers of his right hand up her triceps and over her shoulder, pausing before continuing up her neck and along her jawline. The sweetest, gentlest brush, but it set off a cascade of need that flooded her veins. She whimpered and leaned into him harder as her knees jellied.

"Though it's hot as hell pinned up, too," he said. "All this skin for me to play with."

A finger sketched a tantalizing line down a tendon in her neck. Desire pulsed between her legs and she shifted against his muscular body. "Zach, what are you doing? I thought we agreed on once."

"We did. And it's been a long week. One where we should have been talking instead of you ducking me at every opportunity—"

"I didn't duck, I—"

"True. You didn't need to duck. You were never in the same place as I was."

His hands settled on her waist and the thin material of her dress felt flimsy. An insufficient barrier.

"I've hurt you too much," she said. The backs of her eyes went prickly hot. "And the more time we spend together, the more I'll keep doing it…"

His fingers tightened on her hip then relaxed as he exhaled slowly. A whisper of a kiss, the barest of brushes, sent shivers down her spine.

"Tell you what," he said. "Let me worry about me. I'll tell you if you hurt me. And the only thing you're doing that's hurting me is avoiding me. Yeah, I've got issues with you dropping me as a client—I think we're a different case from what would normally apply to your code of ethics. But I'm not going to let you drop me in any other way. We've tried avoidance. We've failed. And I refuse to fail you."

What—what did that mean? Her brain stuttered. "I don't know what you're asking me for."

"Right now? Nothing." He made a noise as if he were just remembering something, and his fingers teased their way down to the hem of her dress. He walked them along her thigh, gathering the short skirt until his palm lay hot on her leg. "Actually, I'm asking you to let me make you feel good. This is supposed to be a happy day and you're looking way too sad. Beyond that, we'll talk later."

His hand slid to her midline, pausing just as his thumb brushed the edge of her panties.

"Anyone could walk in," she protested.

"I flicked the latch."

She moaned at the little mimicking motion he made, twitching his pointer finger along the sensitive flesh of her upper thigh.

"There's a double entendre in there somewhere, but that doesn't seem like our style," she said.

"You want me to flick your latch, Cadence?" he teased, finally bringing his hand to rest on her mound. With a finger on either side of her panties, he traced torturous lines, coming so close but not close enough.

"Mmph," she let out, melting against his chest.

"That a yes, *belleza*?" He nudged the edge of her underwear and dipped a finger between her folds.

"Zach—" She bit her lip and wiggled against his hips. A hard ridge proved she wasn't the only one needing release.

"I want the words. Yes?"

"Yes."

He plunged his fingers further, filling her to the threshold of sanity. She bit her lip and stifled a cry. She didn't know where this was going and she definitely didn't want anyone else to know they were having the conversation.

Not that this involved talking. Though if she wasn't careful, his giving fingers, coaxing out her pleasure dangerously fast, would have her begging.

"This position leaves something to be desired," he grumbled. With him at her back, she couldn't see him, but given their height difference he had to have his knees bent.

It downright hurt to jar his hand away, but she didn't want him to end up with a leg cramp. She turned, bringing herself face-to-face with smoky green eyes and a jaw set in determination. Rising on her toes, she tasted him, a quick sample, just enough to get the heady flavor of him on her tongue. It had only taken once for her to learn it. And it would only take a few more seconds for her to get addicted.

But pulling away, walking out of the pantry without slaking her consuming arousal, was not an option.

He nipped at her lower lip before gripping her hips and lifting her onto the freezer.

Plastic chilled the backs of her bare thighs. "Wh-what are you doing?"

"I figure we're going to be missed in about two minutes. Clock's ticking." He knelt and, one at a time, lifted her legs, draping her calves over his broad shoulders. He pushed her underwear over. "Much—" his breath teased her sensitive flesh and she pressed her lips together and whimpered "—much better."

Her spine melted. She reached back and clung to the hinge-edge of the freezer. "It'll do," she mumbled.

"Oh, *it'll do*, she says." Roughened thumbs brushed her sex and he pressed his tongue to her, sending her soaring toward the edge of her control. "How about that?" he said, words muffled but tinged with humor. "Will that do?"

"It might in about three sec—"

"If you can still count, I am *not* doing my job." He flicked his tongue and another wave of heat flooded her body.

"Mmm," she breathed, tilting her pelvis, angling so the touch of his greedy mouth went from perfect to sublime and the edges of her vision went fuzzy. She could seriously spend the rest of her life with Zach Cardenas's head between her thighs.

The rest of her life?

"You're thinking again, Cadence."

"I—"

"Think later."

"Zach—"

Spreading her thighs wider, he thrust his thumbs into her heat.

She cried out and dissolved on him, her limbs going limp as a shower of bliss consumed her body, her mind.

Her heart.

Chapter Twelve

Zach's chest heaved as he carefully unwound Cadie's shapely calves from around his neck and shoulders. Shifting her underwear back in place, he straightened her skirt and stepped between her legs. He slid his hands to her lower back and pulled her toward him, landing a kiss on the tender skin just below her earlobe.

The dazed, sated look on her face topped the gold medal he'd won on home soil. He'd retired after those games. Stopping at the peak had seemed prudent. But he and Cadie were nowhere near their peak. And he didn't want to stop receiving the gift of her soft lips pressed against his collarbone as she breathed through the aftereffects of her release.

Hiding away in her father's pantry and making her dissolve on his face, however, did not a relationship make.

Man, Caleb had been right—her needs mattered exponentially more than the promises he'd made to Sam. But that didn't mean the promise didn't matter at all. Sure, Zach's heart skipped at the possibilities of getting to wake up next to Cadie every morning, of teaching

Ben how to ride a tricycle or properly ski a zipper line down a mogul run.

But could he do all those things without erasing Sam?

"We've been gone too long," she croaked. "People are so going to know what we were doing. And you didn't even get the chance—"

"I'll be fine," he said, chuckling. "We'll worry about me next time. I'm betting you're good for it."

Her fingers dug into his shoulders and she drew in a shuddering breath.

"I really want there to be a next time," he said.

"How?" The word came out with an edge of anguish that cut through him like a cold knife blade. "I'm not the risk taker I used to be. I look into our future and all I see are massive, immovable barricades. My issues, Sam—" She swore. "What would everyone say?"

He froze. No, she wasn't the woman she'd been before she lost Sam. The nasty fears she'd obviously developed about loss wouldn't disappear overnight. But he loved her. Loved Ben. Fragments of logic consolidated into a gleaming whole and lightness buoyed his chest until he felt like he could catch air without a jump. Could grab her hand and leap right over any barricades she was struggling to clear.

Leaning back enough to be able to see Cadie's face, he stroked the underside of her chin with a finger. The pain that had sliced ribbons into her voice was pooled in her eyes, leaving them a dull blue-gray. He hated that she'd lost her bliss the minute he'd suggested they seek out something more than a tear-your-clothes-off rendezvous.

"Let's think about this, *belleza*. Yeah, some people might fuss over us getting together, but it's really only our business. And the last thing I want to do is step into Sam's shoes. But, Cadence—" He rubbed a circle over the soft cotton of her dress, just above the curve of her bottom. "You're a different person than when you were married to Sam. You have different needs, different expectations— you need a different guy. I won't be taking Sam's place."

What was the word his therapist had used when she'd worked with him on his survivor's guilt? Reframing? That was a hell of a reframe.

Stiffening, she stared at him and let go of his shoulders to fuss with the skirt of her dress. "You told me you didn't think you could be with me."

"I did," he said. *Honesty time.* He palmed her shoulders and dropped his forehead to her crown, inhaling the scent of fresh air and cherry shampoo. "I was wrong. I just want to find a solution, some balance that'll let me be with you without betraying Sam."

"Oh, great." Pain flared on his ribs as she jabbed him with a finger. "You can't change the rules, Zach. I invited you to stay on Saturday because I thought we were on the same page. You couldn't do more. I couldn't do more. But now you're saying you can?"

"I'm saying what we think is in our way might not be in our way—"

She placed a hand against his chest, forcing him back a few inches. His heart ached that she wanted to put space between them. The distance felt wider than the Gallatin National Forest.

"You think Sam's the problem," she said dully.

"Well, yeah…" He took a shuddering breath. "He doesn't have to be, though. We could find something new. You could keep the memories you have with him. And I can be something different for you—"

"Sam's not the problem, Zach."

"He is for—"

"You," she spat, the rosy glow of pleasure vanishing

from her cheeks as she turned as white as the freezer beneath her. "For you. I get that. But not for me."

Blinking in confusion, hating that she obviously didn't want him to comfort her despite the tears dampening her eyes, he dug a hand into his hair. "I don't understand."

Her face softened. "I know."

"Sam's *not* the problem," he repeated, trying to jam that square peg of a concept into the round hole he'd assumed to be the truth.

Breathing slowing into something that sounded like a purposeful, soothing rhythm, she studied him. "I'm the problem."

"How?" She seemed like the answer to everything wrong in his life. And for a moment he thought he'd found a solution.

"I'll never be able to do *this*."

Talk about taking him out at the knees. He actually grabbed the shelf at his back to keep himself steady. "I'm sorry?"

She reached out to steady his elbow, a professional veneer covering the raw emotion in her blue eyes. "You should sit down."

"I don't need to sit. I need you to explain what you meant." The words came out sharper than he'd have liked, so he gentled his tone. "Sorry. Can you explain?"

"Maybe?" Self-doubt crossed her beautiful features and she glanced to the side. "I don't want to be in a relationship, Zach."

"With me, yeah, I'm getting that."

She shook her head vigorously enough that a strand of dark hair fell from her messy topknot. "No, I don't want to be in a relationship with anyone."

His throat thickened. "I see."

"Do you?"

He lifted a shoulder. "Hard not to understand. You've lost more than most people have at a young age. Being scared to risk again makes sense. It could have just as easily been me caught in that avalanche."

"It's not the risk," she said, staring at him with knowing eyes. "Your job and all that—it doesn't bother me."

"What does?" he said, hearing the gravel in his voice.

"Love." Her lip wobbled. "I loved Sam. And he loved me. And we still fell apart."

"I know, but…" He brushed her cheek with a thumb. She flinched. Chest clenching, he dropped his hand. "We all have our faults. But the problems you ran into with Sam… I don't think you and I would have that same—"

"Did Sam ever mention wanting a divorce?"

"He—" Goddamn it. This was not the moment he wanted to talk about his argument with Sam. Yeah, he'd promised himself, promised her, that if she ever wanted to know, he'd tell her. But *now*? If he confessed that the night before the avalanche Sam had been talking divorce, it would only confirm her trust issues. "Can we talk about this later?"

She threw up her hands. "You can't even be honest with me. How can you tell me you'd be any different from Sam?"

His face went numb as the blood drained from his skin to pool, hot and throbbing, in his gut. "Cadence."

"What?" she bit out.

"I love you…"

"If that's true—"

"*If* that's true?"

"If that's true," she repeated with a deadly calm, "then back off."

"But—"

"Was it the *back* or the *off* that didn't make sense?"

she said, voice rising with each word. She shoved off the freezer and headed for the door. "I need to return to the party."

He caught her elbow. "I'll answer your question, just like I promised. But not while we're angry and not while you should be enjoying Ben's day. So as soon as you want to listen, let me know." Jamming his fists in his pockets to keep himself from taking her hands and falling to his knees to beg her to change her mind, he slid the pocket door open for her. "And I'm not going to stop loving you. It doesn't work that way."

I'm not going to stop loving you...
Three days had passed since Ben's birthday and no matter what Cadie tried, Zach's words still rang in her head.
It doesn't work that way...
That was the problem. It *did* work that way.

Sam had fallen out of love with her, and she with him. She couldn't count on a partner to stick around. And given Zach apparently knew more about Cadie and Sam and the ugliness that had gone down around her pregnancy, she didn't understand why he was so adamant that she and him would be different. They'd eventually fall away from each other, too.

Her attempts to distract herself had failed. Yesterday she'd invited Lauren over for a movie-and-popcorn night and had spent the entire film fantasizing about Zach instead of the remarkably delicious hero.

And today the Tuesday Evolve management lunch meeting was mind-numbing. Current and projected registration numbers bounced out of her head faster than Lauren could recite them. She caught on to enough to see they were operating in the black, but the specifics were lost in the ether. It was as if she was Charlie Brown and the rest of the gang at the table were the adults.

Wah-wah-wah-wah-wah.

"Do you think he'd be up for being a part of some advertising, Cadie?" her sister asked.

She gave her head a shake, trying to clear the cobwebs. "Huh? Sorry. I was…"

An excuse didn't come quickly enough and Lauren rolled her eyes. "It's okay. But penance for spacing out on me—you have to ask him."

She sighed. "I have to ask what of whom?"

"Zach. He's brought a ton of business our way and, between working with you last month and Deon now, he's looking ripped as hell. Think he'd be willing to be the gym's poster boy?"

Cadie wanted to flat-out refuse but too many people were watching her: Lauren; Garnet as the representative of the holistic practitioners; and the managers of the spa, gym and juice bar. The gym manager's eyes were especially bright at the prospect. Understandable. Any male-loving resident of Sutter Creek would likely get behind having Zach Cardenas's pecs plastered across bus stop shelters and on the local business foldout of the *Sutter Creek Sentinel.*

She groaned internally. She'd never get away from her desire for him were that the case.

"I really don't see him going for it," she hedged.

"Gotta ask," Lauren announced. "Deon was saying that he had Zach carving some basic turns on the ski simulator the other day—Zach might be pumped enough by his progress that he'd be willing to let us have a few choice shots."

"Good grief. Pimp out your own man, Lauren."

Oh, crap. Cadie swallowed her horror. *Your own.*

Implying Zach was hers.

"I didn't mean—"

Matching expressions of amusement danced on Lauren's and Garnet's faces. The rest of the team seemed unfazed, but her sister and friend were choking back laughs.

"I'm sure Tav would love the vote of support on his hotness, but we need him behind the camera, not in front of it," Lauren explained.

"We'll see," Cadie blurted, her nerves clamoring for a subject change. "Next topic?"

They finished a half hour later and Cadie slammed her folder shut and darted out of the conference room.

"Hold up, grumpy pants!" Lauren called right before Cadie could duck through the PT facility's back entrance.

Cadie stopped. Resting her back against the hallway wall, she looked to Garnet, who stood next to Lauren, for support. "Grumpy pants?"

"I'll second that," Garnet said, tugging one of her loose red curls and wrinkling her nose in apology.

"It's gotten even worse since Ben's party," Lauren insisted. "When I saw you disappear with Zach, I thought—"

"Stop," Cadie bit out.

"I'm just saying," Lauren said, not following orders. "Step one, you were sad. Step two, mysterious disappearance. Step three, you're tousled. And extra sad. So something happened—"

"Isn't moving supposed to be in the top ten stressful life events a person can go through?" She wasn't going to mention that losing a spouse was number one. She'd already played that card.

Lauren waved a hand. "Not even close. It's like number twenty-three or something."

Curse her sister's medical and sociology background. "Give me a few days, I'll be fine."

"You're sure it's not that you got your freak on with Zach somewhere in Dad's house?"

Cadie's cheeks got hot and she glanced up and down the hallway to make sure her humiliation was being witnessed by Garnet and Lauren alone. She owed it to Zach not to spill their secrets. "I'm just stressed because of moving, and parenting, and work…"

"Hon," Lauren murmured, "we all get that you've taken a lot on. Single parenthood alone isn't for the faint of heart and then with Evolve—"

"Which is doing fine," Cadie snapped.

She must have looked close to her breaking point because Garnet stepped closer and rubbed her arm.

"Then why are you so touchy?" Lauren asked.

She threw up her arms. "It would be nice to feel like I have everything under control! For a few minutes at least. But… I don't." Odd that she could admit that easier than how, yes, they'd gotten almost all the way around the bases on Saturday. And that had ended with Zach spilling his soul to her and she sucked so badly as a human being that she'd had to squash his earnest attempts for them to be together. Tears pricked her eyes.

Garnet put an arm around her. "No one has it all together, Cadie."

"Thanks." Cadie sniffled and squeezed back before stepping away. "It's stupid, I know. Youngest-child syndrome."

Lauren snorted. "Uh, pretty sure you're not the only one in the family who's struggled to keep it together."

Warmth spread in Cadie's chest at the reminder that her sister had made her fair share of mistakes recently, had stuck with a career she'd hated for far too long in a misguided attempt to please their father. Lauren's graciousness deserved some more honesty.

"Zach was supposed to be my success story. But it wasn't working and passing him off was—" *humiliating* "—frustrating."

Lauren and Garnet shared a long, curious look with each other but seemed to silently agree to let that go, because they both nodded.

"I think we can call this place a success," Lauren said. "And you know you were a massive part of that."

Cadie pressed the heels of her hands into her eyes. "It's not just Evolve. I'm *afraid.* And I don't want to be afraid anymore."

"Oh…" Her sister sucked in a breath and then hugged her tightly enough to cut off Cadie's airflow.

"Right. Okay. Change the subject," Cadie ordered, wriggling out of her sister's arms.

Garnet clapped her hands together. "If you *do* want to boost sales, getting Zach's picture up around town is not going to hurt." She peered into the rectangular window of the physical therapy door. "He's right there. You can ask him about the ad campaign."

"Start small with the fear." Lauren poked her in the side. "Which with Zach would mean going on a date. However, if you're not ready to follow your heart, at least ask him about modeling for us."

Good God, she and Zach were so far beyond dating. But she had to keep up appearances to keep her sister off the trail of the truth. "You're still trying to push him and me together? And while we're at work? Seriously?"

"Oh, as if Garnet hasn't picked up on the sexual tension between you two. It's as thick as the ice-cream cake you served at Ben's party."

Frowning, Cadie glanced at Garnet for confirmation.

Her friend lifted a "gotta concede that one" shoulder.

"I'm not asking Zach out on a date." Cadie breathed deeply. "But you have a point about the small steps. I'll see what he says about being objectified for profit."

Gulping, she pushed through the door. Lauren and Garnet tumbled after her.

Zach was the only person in the workout area and he eyed them carefully as they approached.

"The Three Musketeers?" he asked dryly. He lowered into a squat, a bar propped on his sculpted shoulders.

"These two have an idea," Cadie said, jerking her thumb toward the other women, "and they roped me into being the mouthpiece."

"You daydreamed your way into being the mouthpiece," Lauren retorted.

Zach eased into another squat and Cadie stared at a spot on the wall to avoid salivating over his muscular thighs. His black shorts left nothing to the imagination, tightening over his ass and hugging his crotch. Not that she needed any more evidence of that glory—she'd be hard pressed to find anyone to live up to Zach in the bedroom.

Flames licked at her neck and she rubbed at the prickly hot skin, praying her reaction to the memory of him ruining her for other sexual partners wasn't showing on her face.

"Mouthpiece for what?" he said.

"For you modeling for us," Cadie grumbled.

Lauren nudged her. "Way to sell it, there, sis."

"For you modeling for us," she repeated in a falsely cheerful tone.

Laying the bar on the floor, Zach shook out his limbs. "Modeling?"

"A few pictures advertising the fitness facility," Cadie explained, sending him an apologetic smile.

Zach linked his fingers together and rested them on top of his head, highlighting the delineations in his biceps.

"That pose would do," Lauren said, grinning.

Zach seemed to all of a sudden find the ceiling fascinating—his eyes fixed on the white tiles. "Creeper," he said lightly, still not looking at any of them straight-on.

Cadie had to lick her lips to get the moisture going again. There was only so much thigh and biceps a girl could take. "It would be a good marketing move for Evolve," she conceded.

"Then I'll do it," he said.

"You will?"

"Cadie." He closed his eyes. Unhappy shadows hollowed the angles of his face. "For a smart woman, it's taking you an absurdly long time to figure out I'd do anything for you."

Twin gasps filled the air as Lauren and Garnet stammered out excuses and bolted back out into the hallway.

Cadie couldn't gasp. She could barely breathe. Her palms dampened. Why would he admit that in front of people like that? How were they supposed to hide if—?

"You can't be surprised." The ache in his tone sliced through her defenses.

"'Anything' is a big promise."

"And seven years is a damn long time to love a woman." Dismay crossed his face, a clear *what the hell did I just say?*

Seven years? Her knees started to shake and she stumbled backward, landing on her rear on a box jump. "That's an exaggeration, right?"

"I wish."

"But…"

He crouched in front of her for a second before shaking his head and sitting on the floor, hooking his elbows around his knees. "Tell me about it. Nothing like lusting over your best friend's wife during their wedding ceremony to give you a complex."

Best friend's wife.

She gulped. "Did Sam know?"

He glanced to the side.

"He knew?"

"He suspected. The night before he died, we argued."

"About what?"

Staring at the space between his knees, he shook his head. "I guess it's time."

"For what?" she asked.

"You accused me of not being honest the other day."

Her heart sank. "I'm sorry. You've been nothing but and—"

"No, I promised I'd tell you the minute you wanted the whole story." Lifting his head, he pierced her with an agony-filled gaze. "You asked if Sam was committed to being a dad. And right after the accident, yeah, he had. But the night before? He was saying the opposite. Nothing I tried could get him to see reason. We had a brutal blow-up. We both accused each other of being out of line. And the next day I was avoiding him. Part of the reason I wasn't there when…"

"Oh." No wonder he'd promised Sam so much.

The pads of her fingers slipped on the edge of the box, making a creaking sound against the painted wood. A pang echoed in her chest. But the deep, gut-wrenching pain she would have expected to feel never arrived. She'd known. Intuition or whatever, something hadn't rung true about Sam's final words. And to an extent, it justified her mixed feel—

No. *Nothing* justified that ugliness.

"I'm sorry, Cadie." Zach slowly shook his head. "I didn't know what to do. Telling you seemed cruel. Keeping it from you didn't seem right, either. And the fact you told me you didn't want to know... I clung to that for a long while."

"You told me at the right time," she mumbled. "I can handle it now." Could she handle his own admission, though? She pressed her fingers into her eyelids. "Seven years?"

"Yeah."

The breath skittered from her lungs. He'd loved her *longer* than Sam. She covered her face with her hands and let out a noise that encompassed some of her confusion and her frustration. But as if a grunt or groan or whimper could properly address *seven years*. If he'd kept loving her all that time, assuming she'd never be free to love him back, what were the chances he'd stop now?

"Hey," he said quietly. She heard him shuffle forward on his knees. Cupping her covered face, he stroked the backs of her hands with his thumbs. "I shouldn't have mentioned that. I didn't mean to pressure you."

"I don't know what to say."

"That's okay." He cleared his throat.

She dropped her hands to look at him. Sincere devotion turned his eyes a rich green. Wow, she was the worst person in the world. Guilt churned in her stomach.

"Zach."

"Really. I've had forever to think about this. Take the time you need."

A breath shuddered from her lungs. "You're too patient."

"You're worth it." The fervent kiss he pressed to one of her palms set her pulse racing.

Was she worth it? She didn't know. But it was time to try to be.

Chapter Thirteen

Zach gripped the rock face of Wild Life Adventures's beginner crag hard enough to leave dents. But neither the exertion from the climb nor the endorphins from doing one of the sports he loved again burned off his tension. It had been building since he'd confessed to Cadie how long he'd been in love with her. When he'd told Cadie to take the time she needed, he'd thought she'd mull over her feelings for a few days. Not *twelve*. His determination to give her space was growing mighty thin.

"Hey!" Andrew's raised voice echoed from the base of the wall where he was belaying Zach's climb. "You stuck up there? Need anything?"

Eh, just your sister for the rest of my life. No big deal. "Yeah, my ever-loving pride back."

"You're golden, Cardenas. And head left—that route's always done well for me." A solid out, given Andrew had watched Zach climb here a good fifty times last summer and knew Zach had the hand and toeholds memorized.

Zach cleared his mind of Cadie and hoisted himself

once, twice, until he was five feet from the top of the crag. Another grab and he had his hand on the ledge.

"One more, man!" Andrew yelled. "You got this!"

Zach scrambled up the remaining distance, neck hot from embarrassment, not exertion. He sat on the edge and glared down at his friend. "I don't need an effing cheerleader."

"Give yourself a break." Rope still in one hand, Andrew propped his other on a hip and squinted upward. "And give me one, too. I've got a lot invested in you not almost-dying again. How are you feeling?"

"Physically? Fine."

Andrew's expression turned puzzled. "And otherwise?"

"Also fine. What else would I have to stress about?"

"My sister?"

"Your sister is Tavish's problem."

"The other one, smartass."

Zach's chest started aching as bad as his throbbing thigh muscles. "Yeah, well, nothing's going on there."

Yet. I just need to bide my time. Andrew drew back in surprise. "Thought I saw something between the two of you."

"Way off base."

"Liar."

"I assure you—"

"Word to the wise," Andrew interrupted. "Next time the two of you sneak off for shenanigans in the middle of a goddamn birthday party, fix your hair afterward, champ."

Zach held a middle finger out over the ledge so Andrew couldn't miss it. "The 'don't ask, don't tell' policy you and I had going on was working fine for me."

"Don't think it's working for her, though," Andrew called up.

Concern shot through Zach's abused limbs. "Why?"

A shoulder lifted. "Something's off. You talked to her lately?"

"Not about anything important." For starters, her thoughts about the fact he'd been head-over-ass for her since the minute he'd caught sight of her precious smile in that skeezy Steamboat bar. He wouldn't mind an answer to that. Say, the same way a fallen hiker stranded in a crevasse wouldn't mind a rescue. "Enough yabbering, jerkface. Hoist me down."

Andrew shook his head but beckoned with a ready signal.

Zach took a deep breath and mentally prepared himself for the pain of descent. No matter how gently he flexed his feet while rappelling, the bouncing was still going to jar.

"Take it slow," Andrew cautioned.

Rewarding his friend with a drawn-out curse, Zach checked his ropes and began his descent. *Take it slow.* Andrew had meant that when it came to rappelling, but it applied to Zach's situation with Cadie, as well. He'd taken it glacial over the last few weeks. *Just a little more patience.*

As he made his way down the rock his options jarred loose. He could let the silence go on for even longer and watch their chance at love wilt away. Or he could break his promise and ask her for her thoughts.

It took little time to descend and Andrew clapped him on the back when he landed. "Good to see you back, buddy. Want to celebrate? Mix things up and head for the Moose instead of the lounge?" he said, referring to the lovingly dilapidated local bar that the townies favored.

"Sure," Zach replied as he unclipped his harness and began winding ropes and removing gear. Maybe he needed to give Andrew's methods a try with Cadie. A change of scenery might work, too. And he had just the place to take her.

"Drew," he said cautiously, "I want to invite Cadie along on the memorial trip."

The breath Andrew let loose gusted enough that Zach half expected to see the branches of the nearby stand of pines flutter. "Serious?"

"Yeah."

"You think she's ready?"

"I—" He kept his gaze low as he fastened the buckles on the harness hanging from his fingers. "No, she's probably not. But she needs a nudge. Get over her fear of loss."

Andrew blinked, his irises so similar to Cadie's that it made it hard to maintain eye contact. "Another thought— you could try not to kill yourself on the job this season."

Zach snorted. "I'll add that to the to-do list."

"Watching you cartwheel down Hammond's Chute was the single most frightening moment of my career." Andrew scrubbed his mouth with a hand. "Because I was petrified for you, sure. But also for Cadie. If anything had happened to you, it would have destroyed her."

Okaaaaay… His friend had never admitted *that* before. Zach arched a brow. "Losing Sam didn't destroy her."

"You're not Sam."

True, but it didn't seem to matter to Cadie. Taking a deep breath, he fiddled with the screw lock on a carabiner. "I hate that I worried her with my fall. Nor can I shake the feeling I could have changed the outcome of that avalanche."

Andrew scoffed and then sobered. He must have realized Zach hadn't made that admission lightly. "No damned way were you responsible for that slide. Come on. You know the science of it too well to take that on your shoulders."

And hearing it from the mouth of a guy he'd watched bomb many an unstable cornice during avalanche control brought that truth home. His limbs tingled. He'd been unable to shake the mantle of responsibility since he'd heard that bowel-loosening rumble of the slope giving way. But Andrew's confidence carried far more weight than when his counselor had tried to convince him he wasn't to blame for any of the tragedy.

"So you think I should ask Cadie up to Whistler?"

Andrew straightened, his relaxed expression falling into seriousness. "What do *I* think? Yeah, it would make sense for her to go."

Resolve filled Zach to buoyant. "I agree. I should—"

"Cadie, though?" Andrew continued as if he hadn't cut Zach off. "I don't think she'll go for it."

For once the doubt bounced off him, didn't sink below his skin. "She doesn't have to. But I'm going to ask anyway." He slung his gear over his shoulder and jerked a nod at his friend. "Rain check on that beer."

Cadie's phone beeped with an incoming text as she heaved Ben's running stroller out of her trunk and flipped it into the open position. Setting the lock, she grabbed her phone out of her pocket.

Zach: Where are you?

Instead of replying with an emotionally honest "hiding from my feelings," she went with the physical truth. Running on the lake trail, she replied then dropped her phone in the handle caddy and retrieved Ben from his car seat. Zach was out climbing with Andrew, so it wasn't like she needed to be worried he'd come find her. Good thing, too. One of these days he was going to press her concerning his little *I've had a thing for you for seven years* announcement. And she still didn't know if she could make her lips form the words "I love you, but I'm afraid that won't last."

"Ready for a jog, sweet pea?" she said to her son as she bounced him on her hip.

Ben strained in her arms, reaching for the general direction of the lake and the beach off the main parking lot. "Wa! Wa!"

"I know, baby. Water. Want to go to the beach after my run?" She clipped him into the stroller. "Let's do that."

The screen of her phone lit up next to her water bottle.

East or westbound?

She glanced to each side of Moosehorn Lake's main public beach. The trail skirted the parkland side of the lake. The east branch culminated at the water-skiing course near her sister's house and the west at another, smaller park. Ben's vote, were his vocabulary made up of more than single syllables at this point, would have been for the latter direction.

West, she typed and then put her phone on silent. She had a hankering for a good long run.

Twenty minutes later she dripped with sweat, having gone full-tilt to the park, where she pushed Ben on the swing and enjoyed the hint of late September crispness riding the air. The leaves were turning red on the trees surrounding the small clearing. Only ten days until Zach headed out for his Whistler trip. Based on Deon's observations, Zach was more than physically ready. She hoped he found what he was emotionally looking for, too. Maybe figured out a way to say goodbye. He deserved to move on.

So do you.

Ignoring her prodding conscience, she pushed her son higher, praising his bravery and grinning as he squealed with glee.

She jogged slower on the return trip, taking time to wave at the few people she passed instead of the curt nods she'd been doling out on her initial leg. At about the halfway point a familiar, exercise-mussed head came around a bend.

Seriously? He *had* intended to track her down?

Zach's long stride ate up the trail as he neared. He smiled at Cadie and immediately squatted down to greet Ben when she stopped.

"Hi, buddy. Did *Mutti* take you to the park?"

Ben let out a long string of babbling.

"Eloquent." Zach grinned and straightened. "No need to stop. I can jog with you."

"You came a long way for ten minutes of running," she ground out as she resumed her easy 10K-an-hour pace. Zach fell into rhythm beside her. She could sense him reining in his strides, keeping back some of the energy of his powerful limbs. She could have picked it up, matched his capacity. But she didn't need to prove herself to him. Somehow she'd always been enough with Zach.

Another tally to add to the *figure out a way to be with him* column.

Contentment softened his features as he tilted his head and made a hand gesture, wordlessly offering to push Ben. She passed off the stroller. It eased her worries to have him holding on to the stable contraption. He looked even on his feet, but it was easy to roll an ankle on a root or—

"You're watching me through your work goggles," he murmured.

She blinked as a little extra warmth, beyond the exertion of her run, rushed into her cheeks. "Uh, I was just wondering how your climb went."

"Just fine."

He really was recovered. He'd have no problem with hiking to the slide site next weekend, or with tearing up the slopes on opening day... Her stomach shifted and a grimace broke through despite her best efforts to hold it in.

"What?" he asked.

She lifted a shoulder and focused on the trail ten feet in front of her. "I didn't see you through until the end."

"Getting me to look at my rehab from a new perspective got me out of my stubborn rut, and that was all you. Take credit."

She made a face. Speaking of stubborn ruts, she liked the one she'd worn for herself. It was comfortable, sticking to her new normal of taking care of Ben and her family and work and definitely *not* jerking her head in the direction of the secluded pine beside them and convincing Zach to pin her against the rough trunk and kiss her senseless.

Their runners thudded in tandem on the packed earth for a few minutes, with only Ben's cheerful babbling to cut the silence.

Zach cleared his throat. "You know, as ruts go, yours—"

"What the hell!" She skidded to a stop, kicking up a puff of dust. "Are you reading my mind now?"

He slowed and paused, turning the stroller toward

the lake view. Bending down, he pointed at the water and said, "Look, Ben, ducks!" Then he straightened and took a few steps toward her. He stuck his hands into the pockets of his shorts. His voice came out as rough as the trail when he said, "Mentioning a rut in reference to me made me think of *you* playing it safe and—"

"And I was thinking about it, too, Zach."

The corner of his mouth lifted. "That's not a bad thing. Just shows we're in sync."

"And I'm not used to that." A chill swept across her sweaty neck and she crossed her arms over her chest. "I had a lot of things with Sam. Attraction, humor, fun—the proverbial never-a-dull-moment—but I don't think—" her throat tightened "—I don't think we ever truly got each other."

He sucked his upper lip between his teeth before releasing it. The last time she'd seen his lip that pink had been when he'd kissed her on her dad's freezer. Kissed her everywhere. Oh, his mouth… Its talents were something else he could earn a gold medal for.

"I don't think so, either," he finally admitted. "Not really."

"But you and I do," she whispered.

Jerking his head in agreement, he turned to face the lake. He linked his hands behind his back, resembling a private lined up for inspection.

"I've been thinking about what you said," she said.

"Me, too."

"I *want to* be able to go for it. To fall for you all the way…"

"So go for it." He turned back to her, holding out his palms in an invitation to link hands. "I'll catch you, *belleza.*"

She tentatively slid her fingers through his and stared

at how his larger hands dwarfed her smaller ones. "I'm scared."

It wasn't the same fear she'd been struggling with for the last couple of months. He'd been too steadfast since they slept together to keep believing she would lose his friendship or that if they broke up, he'd walk out of Ben's life never to return. But neither of them were going to be happy with indefinite inertia.

He rubbed his thumbs along the insides of her wrists. When he finally spoke, his voice was as stable as the mountain peak visible over the tops of the trees on the other side of the lake. "We'll go slow. Promise."

A breath shuddered from her lungs. His grip, so warm, engulfing hers, begging her to let him take on some of her fear, tightened. She didn't need to worry about him filling his end of the bargain. But could she trust herself? "I don't know what to do, and I hate that."

"I have an idea for what the first step could be," he said.

"We've kinda jumped the gun in a few key areas..."

He grinned. "And well, too. But seriously—what would you think about coming to Whistler with me? For a few of the days, at least."

"Without Ben?" The knee-jerk protest flew from her lips.

"Yeah."

"I—" She was about to claim childcare as a reason not to go, but she stopped herself. Lauren would watch Ben, no questions asked. "Taking off work..."

"Cadie, who's going to be mad at you for going? For finding some closure? You could reschedule your appointments and no one would even blink an eye. Deon would cover anyone who needs to be seen urgently."

"I don't know if I *can* find closure," she admitted. "Like I said, the problem's not Sam, it's me."

"Can you really separate the two?"

Panic gripped her throat. "I sure hope so, because I don't want to feel this way for the rest of my freaking life."

"That's not what I meant." He squeezed her fingers. "I think you owe it to yourself to try."

Ugh, why was he sounding so rational? "What if I get to Whistler and actually boarding the helicopter, going to the place Sam died, is too tough? I don't want to hold you back."

"You won't." The faith in his smile lifted her. "And if you do, you can stay with my parents. Or one of my sisters. Hell, they'll all be scrambling to meet you."

"Easy, killer," she murmured. A lump petrified in her throat. Awesome. Another group of people she'd end up failing if she didn't manage to get her crap in a pile. "I don't think I've technically agreed to date you yet, let alone meet your family."

"They don't need to know about anything between us."

"If your mother has even a bit of maternal intuition— and with four kids and you turning out so great, I'm betting she does—"

"So great? Aw, thanks, honey," he said with a wink, dropping one of her hands to draw his thumb along her cheek.

Ignoring the sparks ignited by his touch, she rolled her eyes. "Anyway, I'm betting she'll figure us out. According to my siblings, we're not good at being subtle."

His lips parted. "So why hide? Why not try being out in the open?"

"Because one part of me wants to grab on to you and never let go. And the other part wants to go hide in the corner at the thought of being with someone else."

"Cadence, I love both parts of you." Cupping her other cheek, he leaned in and brushed his lips to hers for a second. "Tell you what. When you need to go hide in a corner, I'll sit with you until you're ready to rejoin the fray. Just—don't retreat again, okay?"

His sweet offer stole her tongue. "S-sit in th-the…"

"Corner. Symbolically. Or whatever that looks like in reality."

"I can try."

"Like I said, one step at a time."

Her heart up and flipped over. The need to fasten her body to his coursed through her. This man, he was willing to sit with her while she worked through her past. And given she wanted a future with him, she had to take the risk. "Okay, then. Step one would be a plane ticket."

Chapter Fourteen

If the Bozeman-to-Seattle-to-Vancouver flights had been challenging, and driving up the Sea-to-Sky Highway in the passenger seat of Zach's rental car even more daunting, Cadie didn't even have a word for stepping onto the helicopter that was going to take them into the backcountry.

She gripped her armrests and said silent thanks that the *thwop-thwop-thwop* of the rotors, muffled by her hearing protection, meant she didn't have to talk to anyone.

Why was filming scheduled for their first full day? Gritting her teeth, she stared out the helicopter window. Trees and half bare peaks stretched in all directions, similar to the view she saw out her window at home in Sutter Creek. Maybe Zach still considered this home. She should ask him if he ever planned to move back to Whistler, or to Canada. That could cause complications…

Stop finding reasons to create distance. She had Zach's need for emotional connection, not his citizenship, to blame for her elevated heart rate.

They'd arrived in Whistler late last night and had met up in the hotel bar with the handful of other people coming on the trip. She hadn't met any of them before, but they knew she was Sam's widow. None of them had seemed surprised by her presence, but they didn't seem at ease around her, either. Hopefully they didn't feel intruded upon. Or critical of Zach draping an arm around her while they'd shared a round of Scotch.

He'd been oh-so-polite on the way up the elevator, holding her hand, opening doors. Kissing her lightly and, with the expected, "Sleep well," turning and heading to his own hotel room. She'd insisted on her own space, and he'd acquiesced, despite the flicker of disappointment lighting his eyes. Claiming to want to stay with the small crew, he'd declined his parents' invitation of a guest room, instead making plans for them to meet up with his family the following day. *Yikes, so not ready to think about that.*

She glanced at him, occupying the seat next to hers and appearing to watch the helicopter window with one eye and her with the other.

You okay? he mouthed. He reached a tentative hand toward hers and she flipped her palm up in invitation. His grip—a warm, solid anchor that comforted for the rest of the flight—soothed.

A half hour later they stood on a small, ice-crusted field surrounded by still bare summits. The director, one other survivor and the camera operator and sound tech were hiking over to a steep slope a few hundred yards to the west, which was covered by grass and some late-season alpine growth. Using a skeleton crew would keep costs as low as possible given they'd already been up in April, Zach had explained.

His arms hung loose at his sides as he surveyed their

surroundings, a hollow shadow twisting his beautiful face. He cleared his throat. "Doesn't look much like the last time we were here."

"Are you going to be able to get done what you need to?" Despite the lack of new snow cover, the crisp air still nipped at her nose and fingertips. She donned a pair of stretchy gloves and crossed her arms over her ski jacket.

Eyes brightening with moisture, Zach pulled a pair of sunglasses from his pocket and jammed them on his face. "We'll take some shots from the top of the hill and the bottom. Plan is to interview Bernice and me. She couldn't make it for the trip in April, either."

"She mentioned that last night." The woman had been one of the survivors pulled out of the avalanche field, and she hadn't wanted to come back up for the anniversary trip. Too much, too soon.

A sentiment of which Cadie was keenly aware.

Zach was pressing his lips together and pinching the bridge of his nose. A rush of protectiveness and love swamped her, almost knocking her off her feet onto the icy ground.

"What about footage of Caleb?" she asked.

"He doesn't want to finish up the project. And Jeff's not pushing. He has enough from the rest of us." He waved a hand at her. "This way."

But as she trailed behind Zach on uneven ground, her heart hurt for the people involved in the accident. She'd tried the tack Caleb was taking—avoidance—and look how well that had worked for her. No, it was time for her to face things head-on. To try to find the elusive closure Zach had encouraged her to seek. Everyone grieved in their own way. The director and Zach, desperately trying to finish this project to honor the friends they hadn't been able to save. Bernice, who'd needed the extra six months to face her demons. And Cadie herself, looking everywhere for a magic switch to flip, to permit her to get on with her life.

After ten minutes of hiking they stopped just before the slope pitched at a mad angle and set up for interviews. With Zach and Bernice busy on camera, recounting their avalanche experiences and relationships with Sam and the other two skiers who died, Cadie took in the view. The ridge of jagged peaks stretched as far as she could see, fading into an indistinct blue on the horizon. Sam would have loved it up here. He'd lived off fresh air and insane verticals.

"You here, Sam-I-Am?" she muttered, far enough from the filming that no one would hear her.

Nor had Sam heard her. Wind kissed her cheeks and teased the hair at her neck, but nothing of her husband remained on this mountain.

Sweat broke out on her forehead, the sheen quickly chilled by a cold gust. An uncomfortable mix of anger and disappointment tore a raw strip up her spine.

Coming up here might have helped Zach check boxes. Put a passion project in the can for him and his friends. But it did nothing for Cadie.

There was no magic switch.

Zach finished his interview at the base of the hill and the camera turned on a pale Bernice. Backing away, he trudged toward the chunk of granite on which Cadie sat, staring up the hill. Her gaze was locked on the twenty-foot cliff hanging over half the steep incline. The emptiness marking her face pooled like glue in the bottom of his gut. He hadn't expected a smile. Not today, not here. Grief seemed to weigh down the rocks scattered along the hill. But he'd hoped for her to finally achieve a sense of peace. That was the whole point of inviting her along.

Instead she sat, stiff-backed, tearing bits of moss off the boulder.

He hovered next to her, not sure of what to say.

"That was the cliff, wasn't it?" she whispered.

His throat dried out and he had to choke out a, "Yeah."

She dug in her jacket pocket for a second. Hand fisted, lashes wet, she closed her eyes. After a pause she blinked. The ruination written on her features thrashed at his core. Shaking, she flung a tiny object in the direction of the sheer face. It glinted in the sun before hitting a rock with a faint clink and disappearing on the ground.

"Was that your wedding ring?" He couldn't keep the disbelief from his voice.

She looked up sharply. "I don't need it. I saved Sam's ring and my engagement ring for Ben, but my wedding band... Seemed right to leave it here."

"Okay..." He should have been happy for a tangible sign of her moving forward, but the challenge marking her expression gave him pause. The outward letting go didn't seem to be connected to any inward release.

He sighed. The urge to gather her up, for his sake as much as hers, was damn near irresistible. But when he inched closer and reached out, she shied away. Her hesitance rolled over him with the force of the avalanche that had swept over the ground under his feet. "I'm sorry, Cadie. I really thought it would help you."

Rolling a thread of moss between forefinger and thumb, she sighed. "I thought it would, too. Once you mentioned it, I was sure it would be the missing piece. That if I said goodbye, it would be enough."

"And it's not."

The stripes of her thin toque blurred as she shook her

head. "I didn't know what I'd expect to find here. Sam's certainly long gone."

His gut bottomed. He'd almost rather she lied to him. Tell him that the trip had brought her some sense of comfort. Instead it seemed like she was collapsing inward. He nodded slowly and rubbed her back. "That he is."

"Not sure if I thought I'd sense an echo, or what, but I sure didn't expect *nothing*."

"Hey." The desire to show her what he saw when he looked at her pushed against his chest. "Sam might not be here, but you are. Maybe you didn't need to see something from the past. Maybe you needed to see now and what's to come. See that you're brave. And you're fighting."

She exhaled and shifted toward him, cuddling under his arm and resting her face in the crook of his neck.

Encircling her in his embrace, he kissed the top of her head. "What do you need?"

"I don't know."

Acid singed this throat. For the second time in his life, he almost lost his lunch on this mountain. He was out of ideas for how to help her move on.

That's because it can't be your idea.

He took a breath and tightened his hold, losing himself in the scent of cherries. "I love you."

Her lips curved against his neck. "I *do* need that."

"Good. I'm not going anywhere."

That night, Cadie clung to Zach's assertions all through dinner, using them as a mantra to calm the temptation to run back to her hotel room and hide under the covers.

You're brave. You're fighting.

While the waitress distributed bills, Bernice announced, "I'm hitting the town! Celebrating making it to the site and back in one piece. Anyone else joining me?"

Zach, who'd eaten most of his meal with a hand on Cadie's shoulder, as if he was worried she would take off were she not anchored down, arched a brow at her in a silent question.

She shook her head.

He squeezed her shoulder and addressed Bernice. "Tripping the light fantastic Whistler-style isn't anything new for me—I think we'll have a quiet night in."

Toying with the floppy collar of her sweater, Cadie took a centering breath. They could watch a movie on Netflix, maybe, or—

"Zach!" Jeff, the director, said as he settled up his part of the bill. "Marja hasn't seen the outtake reel and some of it's hilarious—want to join us?"

Zach glanced at Cadie again. "Up to you."

Not quite the movie she had in mind, but if she was going to keep fighting… "Sure."

"Really?" he murmured in her ear. "Watching tape of Sam, it's not—"

"It's not easy," she interrupted. "Obviously. But you're the one who called me brave."

He grinned.

Once they were back at the hotel, Jeff plugged his gear into the TV of his suite and they settled in the conversation area, Marja and Jeff in the chairs and Cadie and Zach on the love seat. Her brain whirred. How close should she sit to him? Should they hold hands? What was appropriate? This trip wasn't about them being together. For her, it was about Sam, and for Zach, it was business. She had to assume he'd ski in more films in the future. Twisting her hands in her lap, she looked at him, letting him see her uncertainty.

Don't worry, he mouthed, draping his arm across the back of the couch.

The outtakes were variations on the bloopers from every other film Sam and Zach had ever done. Bails, biffs and dirty jokes.

She nudged Zach with her elbow at a clip of him tumbling down the hill. "Good one, superstar."

"Takes skill to look that good when you're ass over teakettle."

Her smile wavered despite her trying to keep it on. She was still too raw to make an innuendo-laced joke about his skill.

And by the way the corners of his mouth turned down, he knew it.

She focused on the TV again, inwardly cursing the awkwardness of the weekend.

A shot of Bernice startling Caleb and one of the other boarders with the ugly-ass plastic crow mask Sam had packed around to all his films for five or so years pulled a laugh from her. Sam had always sworn that nothing got his films more attention than some well-placed social media hilarity. But then Sam entered the frame. Blond and carefree and cocky—*son of a mother.* She'd been sitting in Colorado, agonizing over her pregnancy and her marriage, and he'd been up on a mountain, mouth stretched in a smile as wide as the slope in the back of the frame.

Anger singed her gut and she couldn't keep her brow from furrowing. There was being brave and then there was torturing herself. And being in Whistler didn't feel like moving forward anymore. Her heart ached to be home with her little boy. To figure out how to make a place in their small apartment for the man desperately trying to shelter her from more anguish. She wasn't going to be able to do that here. After another few minutes of watching, she inched closer to Zach. "I think I'll head back home in the morning. There's a bus to the airport, right?"

"Yeah, but… Hey." He brushed a hand on her soft cheek and the affectionate caress made her eyes sting. He glanced at Marja and Jeff before whispering, "Filming's done early. How often do you get a day to yourself? I'd love to squire you around my hometown. And what about dinner with my parents?"

She clenched her teeth to stop them from chattering together. "This trip isn't turning out how I thought. I don't see the point of staying."

He rubbed his fingertips over his jaw, his expression teetering between concern and losing hope. "I—come on, Cadie. Let's go get a drink, talk about it."

"I didn't mean it that way," she whispered, putting a hand on his knee and gripping. She didn't want him to think she was deserting him. But she had to put her mental well-being first, and that meant being at home. "I'm overwhelmed—"

The music accompanying the outtakes cut abruptly as the feed switched to a new file. Cadie jerked her attention to the screen. An image of Sam and Zach standing under an open-sided tent filled the television. Zach-of-last-year was calmly waxing a pair of skis as Sam stood with his arms crossed over the suspenders of his snow pants.

"What, you think you've got a better answer?" Sam's voice came out angry, ugly, from the speakers. "A kid would ruin my life."

The words coursed through her like an electric shock, pinning her to the couch. *Ruin my life…* She opened her mouth but her tongue was too thick, too dry to move.

Zach stiffened next to her. He stroked her back and

turned to Jeff. "This was recorded? Where's the remote? We should not be watching—"

"Seriously!" Sam's voice elevated through the speakers. "You have opinions? Well, don't hold back."

"Leaving her would be stupid."

Cadie froze at Zach's filmed pronouncement. "Turn it off," she said. "I do not need to hear Sam disagree with that."

Marja scrambled for the volume on the TV remote. Jeff lurched toward his computer, but Zach skipped that step, leaping to his feet and yanking the cords out of the television. The on-screen standoff disappeared, the television glowing a blank purple.

"Better?"

"Yeah, sure." She was better.

Better off without Sam.

She hated that voice, the one that whispered when she was at her most weak and selfish.

But I am—

No! She slapped the thought away. The same way she'd slapped it away at Sam's funeral. It wouldn't budge, spreading in her belly like a sticky oil spill, coating all the decent parts of her. A gurgle of protest escaped her throat and she slapped a hand over her mouth. Three pairs of eyes stared at her. Marja and Jeff, both wincing in embarrassment. And Zach, standing slumped by the television, silently imploring her to… She wasn't quite sure what. His expression was hard to read, making her wonder what he knew.

Yeah, he'd told her about the argument and about Sam's love-and-commitment last words. But had Sam genuinely changed his mind because of the avalanche? Was Zach's recounting accurate? Or had he crafted a half-truth in an attempt to soothe her? Had he covered up what happened that day? Maybe. And maybe she should feel betrayed by that. But it wasn't like she could point fingers about dishonesty. She'd been covering up her true feelings more than anyone.

A heaviness she hadn't felt since her first days of being widowed spread through her limbs. Despite her shaking legs, she managed to stand. "My cue to leave."

Great thing about hotel rooms—even big suites like Jeff's—was the invariably quick trip to the door. She managed to get down the hallway to the elevator without the stinging in her nose dissolving into sobs.

Heavy footsteps followed in her wake. "Wait!"

She jammed the elevator call button. *Arrive already.*

Zach got there first, slamming a palm high up over the closed crack of the metal doors. "Cadence…"

She turned to him, unable to give him more than a blank look because if she let a fraction of emotion show, she'd crack, flood, and that wasn't happening in public. "Give me a minute."

"Belleza." He reached a hand out and she dodged the attempt at a soothing gesture.

"That's *not* giving me a minute."

Heart begging her to escape Zach's handsome, panicked face, she headed for the stairs instead, rushing down the two flights with him following, steady and solid as always. A band of grief cinched around her chest and she struggled to get in the air necessary to keep moving. By the time she reached her hotel room, her breathing was reduced to gasps. Vision blurred, she kept missing as she aimed her key card toward the slot in the door.

"Oh, come on," she muttered. Beads of sweat pricked her neck and tears stung her eyes.

Zach settled a hand on her lower back and plucked the

card from her fingers. His hand shook, too, but he managed to get the door open on the first try. "I'm so sorry—"

"What do you have to be sorry about? You're not the one who feels *relieved* that your husband died!" And as the words rushed out, all the effort it had taken her to keep going for the last year and a half drained into a pool at her feet. She clapped her hand over her mouth as her dinner burned upward. Launching herself toward the bathroom, her gut lurched and she just made it to the toilet in time to aim at the bowl.

Chapter Fifteen

"Cadence, honey." Pain jolted up Zach's bad leg as he landed on his knees beside her and gathered her hair at her neck. He'd selfishly pushed her to come this weekend and it ended with her being so wrecked she puked? Self-loathing rolled through his body.

Gripping her knees, she heaved in a breath. "I'm—I'm done. I think."

He stroked what he hoped was a soothing rhythm on her back. "Breathe. What is it, in for four and out for eight?"

"Something like that." Standing, she stumbled to the sink, plucked her toothbrush out of a glass and smeared toothpaste on it. "This'll fix all my problems," she mumbled around the brush.

"Umm…" He rose to sit on the edge of the bathtub, adrenaline fading into numbness along his skin. He worked his tongue along the dry roof of his mouth. "All of them? Really?"

She spat and rinsed her mouth. "Well, it's preferable to retasting my dinner."

He couldn't bring himself to smile at her attempt at a joke. She'd just made herself sick with guilt. Humor wasn't an option, not when he was still rocking from her words. It was like being hit with one of the howitzer shells they used for avalanche control. She thought relief wasn't a normal part of grief? He had to show her the fallacy in that.

Plunking her toothbrush back in the glass, she made brief eye contact with him through the mirror before fleeing the bathroom.

He followed her to the side of the bed, where she toed out of her flats and climbed under the white duvet, clothes and all. "You should go," she said.

"But…"

"Really."

"You sure you should be alone right now?" He sat down on the opposite bed, waiting for an invitation to get closer. His fingers twitched with impatience and he tented them in his lap.

Her face fell. She waved a hand at him. "Look—you don't even want to touch me!"

His insides hollowed and his mouth fell open. "Are you kidding me?"

"No, Zach, I'm not kidding you." Sniffling, she wiped at reddened eyes with furious fists. She pulled the covers around her chin. "Didn't you hear what I said? Why would you *want* to touch me?"

Well, damn. Shucking his hoodie and boots, he scooted under the covers behind her. Her body curved against his, her muscles shuddering against his front. He wrapped an arm around her middle and buried his nose in her hair, needing a hit of her cherry-sweet scent. "We're going to have to disagree on that one. I've been wanting to touch you all day. But it's been a weird one, and I was trying to pay attention to your cues. Things kept going sideways, though. And then they pitched into the abyss with that video."

She let out a hoarse laugh. "You underplayed the harshness of your argument. But it's not like I've been completely honest with you about everything."

Nerves singed his belly and the need to explain the argument further niggled at him, but instinct told him her concern outranked his. "How so?"

"Come on. You want me to repeat myself?" A breath shuddered from her. "I felt *relieved*—"

"Grief's multifaceted," he pointed out. "I don't see why relief isn't a normal part of the process."

Her slim frame went rigid in his arms. "How can it possibly be normal to feel good about someone being dead?"

"I…" How the hell could he word it differently, get her to believe it?

"When I got the call, I was at work… The rest of that day blurs together, but a few things stand out. I had to book a flight. My coworkers were talking to me, but I didn't understand a word they said. Somehow I stayed upright. Alone. I was in shock, for sure. Shaking from it. But under it all ran a strong sense I'd be okay. That life would be easier. My husband had just died and I was thinking about how much smoother parenting our future child would be!" A keening sob tore from her lungs and she quaked in his embrace.

"Shh. I'm not saying all our grief-related emotions are socially acceptable. But they *are* all normal. Do you know how pissed I was at Sam? And at myself? Months of therapy sessions." Shifting his arm from her middle, he ran a hand down her hair and along her shoulder. "What did your counselor say about it?"

"I didn't tell her."

"Aw, no. You have to. It's not healthy to keep it in."

"You think? But how was I supposed to admit that to another person? Face their disgust?"

"You just told me, and I'm not disgusted." He shook his head. "You're not relieved he's dead. You're relieved you're not together anymore. And you've taken the two feelings and merged them together. In an ideal world, he'd have lived, would have come home. You'd have separated, because you weren't right for each other. Would have co-parented somehow. Or not, maybe. And you would have acknowledged you weren't meant to be together and wouldn't feel badly about that."

She made a choking sound. "Aren't you worried I'm going to feel the same way about you?"

No, because I'm not Sam. Shame bit at the back of his throat. Talk about socially unacceptable feelings. "We're different people with a different dynamic. So, no, I don't think you would end up feeling that way."

"I don't trust myself anymore."

You don't trust anyone. Including me. "I trust you. And I'll keep doing it until you figure out how to feel the same."

She turned over in his arms and stared at him with tear-swollen eyes. The doubt clouding her expression punctured a massive hole in his already deflating sense of hope. Shifting, she touched his cheek with her palm. "You didn't shave today."

"Or yesterday. I'd offer to go deal with it, but I don't want to leave you."

A flicker of desire crossed her face. She hooked a leg over his thigh and circled her hips. "I don't want you to leave, either."

The hard ridge thickening behind the fly of his jeans threatened to take over his thought process. He groaned.

"We have to talk about what was on that video before we do anything involving you moving against me like that."

"Like this?" She pressed her center against his erection.

Damn, he needed her. The high emotion of the day demanded to be drained through physical release. Desire tightened at the base of his spine, urging him to deal with their clothes so that he could thrust into her warm, welcoming body. *No. Self-control, Cardenas.*

"Exactly like that. In a bit. After we talk." His need turned his voice raspy.

She stilled and pressed her lips together, staring at a point over his shoulder. Her face, inches from his, hardened in a way he wasn't used to. "He actually used the words 'ruin my life.'"

Chest seizing, he nodded sharply. And his pushing her to come had forced her to face it.

"Why did you sanitize his feelings so much?"

"I—" He could barely take a breath around the lump of regret clogging his throat. "I didn't want that to be the last thing anyone remembered of him. That he was about to make a reprehensible decision. I can't even—he was a mess after the avalanche. Suffering like I'd never known a person could. But his first thought was for you, that you be safe—I wanted to believe he'd recognized leaving you would be the biggest mistake of his life. When he told me his plan the previous night, I couldn't stand him in that moment. And I wanted to remember my friend as being something better than that. Wanted you to be able to believe in Ben's dad, too."

"Hey." She dragged her thumb on his temple. A wet sensation spread on his skin.

He was crying? Awesome. He blinked, lids hot against his damp eyes.

"Always so honorable." Uncertainty colored her tone.

Crap. What could he say to for her to believe in him? In their future? "I'm sorry I invited you along. I couldn't win either way. Did I support you while you hid or encourage you to deal with it because—" shame dug its claws into his confession, but he forced it out "—because I wanted you for myself? Believed I could be a better husband than Sam had been?"

Her fingers dug into his back. She bit her lip but didn't respond.

He croaked out a bitter curse.

She nodded. "Like you said, not all our grief is socially acceptable, right?"

"I guess." Didn't feel right coming from his end, though. Her feelings had been coping mechanisms. His had been purposeful choices to facilitate being with her.

Do I even deserve this?

Her eyes narrowed. "What are you talking about?"

"Huh?"

"Do you deserve this?"

Ah, hell. "Uh, rhetorical question."

She bit her lip and traced a finger down his jaw. "Something tells me it's absolutely real."

Not knowing how to reply, he kissed her lightly.

"And no, you don't deserve it, Zach. How could being in a relationship with someone who doesn't know how to let go of her past possibly be good for you?"

"You're more than good—you're it for me." He deepened the kiss, but her response was all surface. Lips and tongue moving, slick and purposeful but lacking the tender overlay he craved. Passionate movements without foundation. "I love you."

She rested her forehead against his shoulder and heaved in a breath. "I love you, too."

He believed her. But he needed more than words. "So work with me here."

"Not here. Told you—" she fumbled with his belt buckle "—I'm going home."

A note of finality rode that pronouncement, more than an "I'll see you in a few days" situation. He swore silently as he gripped her waist. "Look, maybe it's not about letting go. Maybe it's about moving forward despite it. Stay. You've shown me your hometown, and I've had a hundred meals with your dad. Let me do the same—"

Pressing a hungry kiss to his jaw, she then ran her tongue along his lower lip, effectively silencing him. Her soft, insistent mouth consumed the rest of his resistance. She tasted like her toothpaste and her light fragrance, sugar and tart fruit, was familiar and all-consuming.

She clearly needed more time to be able to trust, to believe.

Love her as long as she'll let you.

Even if that only meant until she flew back home.

The precise but gentle movements of her hands as she shoved his jeans down suggested building desire but also the need to savor. He lifted his hips to let her get the clothing down to his knees. She hooked a toe in and pushed them off the rest of the way. Her apex brushed his front and his hips tipped into her, the heat of her searing him through her leggings and his boxers.

"I don't want to rush," he said, throat strained. "But, honey…"

She replied by divesting both of them of their clothes in a few seconds and tipping him onto his back. Climbing on, she notched her sweet center over his length.

Hot. Slick. Her body was a damned dream. Her fingers dug into his shoulders and a glassy haze crossed her face, a hint of sexual intoxication playing on her lips. His eyes shuttered closed and he groaned. Need pooled at the base of his spine, a clamoring desire to thrust, to release in her slick passage. Prying his lids open, he reached up and tugged the elastic holding up her hair. Dark brown curls tumbled around her shoulders. He could watch that sweet fall for the rest of his life without tiring of it.

She took his erection in a firm hand and lined them up. Luscious wetness kissed his length and his pelvis bucked. This was going to be off the charts—

She let out a blistering swear word and let go of him.

Huh? Body complaining at her retreat, he reached for her with desperate hands, but she'd scooted off him. "What?"

"We need a condom. I'm not on the Pill."

"Oh, right. Yeah. In my jeans."

Fumbling at the bottom of the bed, she must have hit gold because he heard crinkling foil. As efficiently as she'd removed their clothes, she had him sheathed. A smirk crossed her face as she took her sweet time settling over him again, taking him in inch by inch. Her pleasure peeked behind her clear amusement over being in control. She caught her lip between her teeth and whimpered, and man, he needed to hear that again. Anchoring his palms on her thighs, he thrust the rest of the way and then slowly withdrew. The slow exit and quick buck in earned him another passion-soaked murmur from deep in her chest.

As they continued the perfect rhythm, she leaned in for a kiss, tracing her fingers along his face as if she were trying to imprint the moment—imprint *him*—on her brain so that she'd never forget it. As if she were planning not to—

No. Do not entertain that. This was about them now. He had this moment. And with a gentle flip-and-roll, he cushioned her against the pillows, slotted himself between her thighs and did everything he could to convince her to give him more.

Post-sex tingles—multiple orgasms would do that to a girl—coursed through Cadie's limbs as she lay sprawled under the covers.

Zach, who'd gone to the washroom to deal with the condom, returned and gathered her to his side. She buried her nose against his chest and inhaled the scent of their lovemaking blended with the clean-air freshness still on his skin from their day outside. Somehow it comforted her and sent her off kilter at the same time. Too much of today had been spent in a numb fog. But that video of her husband—*ruin my life*—had blown away the fog and exposed the barren, ugly parts of her psyche she didn't want to face. Shame nudged at the sated edges of her glow. Zach might not be disgusted by her feeling relief over Sam's death, but she still was.

"Hey." The syllable hummed close to her ear. "Those thoughts don't seem like I-just-dissolved-three-times-on-my boyfrie—" He swallowed so hard that her head rose on his chest. The cut-off word clung to the air like stale campfire smoke to a sweatshirt.

"You can say it."

"Can I? Seems we'd need to cross a few more prerequisites off the list before we started using that kind of label."

"Like what?" she asked.

The lack of an answer set off alarm bells.

"Zach?"

His callused fingers rasped against the sensitive skin on her lower back. "I meant what I said when I promised to wait with you while you untangled your feelings. But you not running anymore was equally important."

"I'm here, aren't I? That's not—" But she was planning to leave early. "Oh."

"Yeah."

"I just… Up on the mountain, it did nothing for me, and that pissed me off to no end. And then hearing Sam say I ruined his life—"

"That's not what he said, *belleza*."

Tears sparked and then flooded out, dampening the skin of her temple and his chest. "It's what he meant. And you should be thankful I didn't do the same to you. Almost forgetting a condom. You'd think I'd have learned my lesson."

His body tensed. "Equally my job to remember."

She sniffed. "Last thing I want is to wreck your life, too."

He hooked a finger under her chin and turned her face toward him. "You think us having a baby would be a bad thing?"

"You don't?"

"Hell, no."

Sitting up, pulling the sheet against her, she shivered as cold confusion flooded her veins. "I'd think today of all days I've proved I'm not an ideal partner."

"Ah, that's such—" He didn't voice the obvious curse. He sat up, too, gripping her knee. "I don't want to wait to be together. So while you're healing, I'm sticking with you. Like I said, you're it for me. And if a baby ever entered into the equation, that wouldn't change."

She wiped her eyes on the sheet. "You and your overdeveloped sense of honor."

He arched a brow. "Yeah, I take my promises seriously. And my responsibilities. But having a baby with you would be nothing but a joy. You want to talk regret? Try spending a year wishing you were the father of your best friend's kid. Knowing your friend asked you to take care of the kid, but also knowing that wasn't *carte*-eff-ing-*blanche* to step in as a dad."

The skin at the base of her tongue tightened and another flood of tears threatened to spill. Zach was too good with Ben for her not to imagine him having a child of his own, but… "You'd really want to have a kid with *me*?"

His mouth tilted with dry humor. "Think about it—we'd just be keeping up with family tradition. Tavish and Lauren are dealing with an accidental pregnancy. And I get the impression Mackenzie and Andrew's wasn't all that planned, either."

Family? Holy crap. But even as her fear-ridden gut protested at the word, deep in her heart she knew Zach had been family for a long time. And equally true: she wanted to work toward permanently defining their relationship that way.

"You didn't answer my question," she whispered.

"About having a baby together? I've wanted to since—" He coughed. "Let's just say watching your belly grow when you were pregnant with Ben was all kinds of torture."

She settled a hand on her stomach, missing the sensation of a baby shifting in her womb.

A hot flash of desire darkened the green in his eyes to the color of the rocks in the creek they'd crossed over last night when they'd all walked back from the main village to the hotel at the Blackcomb base.

"It would be early, sure," he admitted. "So no, I'm not asking you if you want to get knocked up tomorrow. But do I want to in the long run? One hundred percent, yes." Reaching out, he ran his knuckles along the back of the hand she still had rested against her belly. "You didn't see the rest of the footage of the argument I had with Sam, but I remember telling him he was off his rocker. That what he had with you was beautiful and rare and he'd spend the rest of his life regretting it if he gave you and Ben up."

Her chest panged. "Not that he got the chance to test that out."

"He didn't, no."

"I—I want to watch the rest of the video."

If he questioned the intelligence of her request, he kept it to himself. Nodding, he kissed her and rose from the bed. "Let me see what I can do."

Fifteen minutes later he came back to the room carrying an iPad. He shucked out of his jeans but kept his T-shirt and boxers on as he rejoined her under the covers. She'd put a tank top and panties on. Despite the comfortable temperature of the room, she shivered and snuggled up to Zach's warmth.

He rested the device on his knees and took her under one of his arms, pressing Play.

Hearing "a kid would ruin my life" was just as ugly the second time around. She glanced up at Zach. He'd closed his eyes and his head was tipped back against the headboard. His words came out of the speaker exactly how he'd told her. *Beautiful...rare...*

That's what a person was supposed to feel about their love.

And Zach had made it infinitely clear he felt that way about her. Warmth spread through her, fighting the tightness in her rib cage caused by Sam's devastating statement.

On-screen, Sam's face changed as he processed Zach's words. Cadie had known her husband's expressions well, and that wasn't the cocky, confident display of a guy happy with his choices. Her husband stacked his hands on top of his head and glared at Zach. She tapped the screen to pause the footage, needing to analyze Sam's face. If she was going to watch this, she was going to get all the answers.

"Man, he was pissed off," Zach mumbled.

"Yeah, but that was a front." She hovered her finger over the tablet, ghosting the lines on Sam's face. "He always scrunched his nose like that when he knew he was wrong but was too stubborn to admit it," she speculated, feeling the same need Zach had to believe the best of her husband.

Zach's eyes were still squeezed shut. She guessed he didn't need to watch it given he'd lived it. "I so wanted to believe I'd gotten through to him."

"He looks pretty miserable," she observed, tapping the tablet again.

"When you're in love, you make it right," came Zach's shout through the speakers. The small size of the recording didn't diminish the men's body language. The creases around Sam's mouth deepened.

And by the rigid set of his shoulders and the way his hands gripped the sawhorse, Zach had been sorely tempted to upend the structure on which his skis rested. "You talk and hash it out until you find common ground. You don't give up, Sam. Love should be selfless. So this isn't turning out how you pictured? Where's your sense of adventure? You sure are brave on the hill, but chicken otherwise. If I had Cadence, I'd move the goddamn Rocky Mountains to see her happy."

"That—" Sam clipped the word with emphasis "—sounds like you've put too much thought into how you feel about *my* wife, Cardenas."

Even through the grainy iPad footage, Cadie saw Zach turn ruddy. "I mean, a woman who loved me like Cadence loves you."

Sam's snort sounded fractured. "You'd be a better husband than me any day."

"A better father, too." Zach had spoken the words so quietly they were barely audible.

The reluctant nod from Sam came through loud and clear, though.

Cadie ripped her gaze from the tablet and stared at Zach. His eyes were open now, fixed on the iPad. His white-knuckled fist pressed tight to his mouth.

The clip went black and Zach moved the device to the side with a shaking hand. He circled that arm around her, holding her tight enough she had to work for breath.

"He did know how you felt. That you loved me," she whispered.

"I'd forgotten some of what we said," he rasped.

"And his admission about your husband-and-father skills—not small, coming from him."

He nodded, his cheek rubbing on the crown of her head.

"So maybe you need to cut yourself a break when it comes to guilt over your relationship with Ben."

"Only if you do the same when it comes to how you felt. Sam knew he had faults. We all do. But grieving isn't one of them. It's just your brain making the best of a brutal situation. It shouldn't dictate the rest of your life."

The lingering numbness cushioning her heart cracked open. It was as if all her nerve endings were exposed, an open cascade along her skin. She curled at the impact and Zach absorbed her movements.

The humanity of it struck her—who the hell didn't have inappropriate reactions? Flaws? Sam's reaction to her pregnancy had been the worst. And he'd chosen wrong. And it was time to ignore the knee-jerk doubt that kicked up every time Zach wanted to get close. She might have poked him about his sense of honor, but he'd been honest with her at the expense of it. So when he'd said Sam had seemed sincere as they'd been packaging him for transport, it was time to believe that.

And she deserved the same benefit of the doubt. Just because Sam had chosen wrong didn't mean she should, too. And staying closed off, not fully engaging with Zach over fear that one of them might screw up and she'd end up alone again… Guaranteed she'd end up alone if she didn't move forward. The worst thing she could do would be to stay numb, stay closed down. Yeah, she and Zach would have the struggles any couple did, would obviously have to work for their relationship like any love worth having. But he'd be there for her and Ben in a way Sam hadn't been. He had Sam's adventurous side, but Zach was more comfortable in his skin, was committed to stability and family.

Peace flooded her body and she melted into the man she loved. "You'd really have stayed with me. Spots and all."

He tightened his arms around her. "I wouldn't 'have stayed.' I *will stay.*"

"I know you will."

A sigh escaped his strong chest. "I'm sensing a 'but.'"

"Nope, no 'but.' It's an 'and' situation. I know you will, *and* I will, too. I know you will, *and* I'm excited to see where love takes us. Together, and as a family. To watch you love my son."

"*Our* son, *belleza…*" Love overflowed from that endearment.

"Right. Ours." But merging their lives would mean

merging more than just the three of them. Her stomach shook. Her family had already wrapped Zach inside its figurative embrace, but would his feel the same toward her? "What are your parents and sisters going to think?"

"That I'm the luckiest guy in the world."

She inhaled a settling breath. "Let's not tell your mom and dad that I wanted to crap out on dinner—on *you*. And I'll try to make them like me tomorrow."

"They'll love you. *I* love you." Growling, he pulled her to straddle his lap. His hungry mouth nipped at hers.

She smiled. The warmth of knowing she was completely loved, completely safe, with this man engulfed her. "Where else are you going to take me tomorrow?"

"Where do you want to go?"

"Whatever you've always loved doing. Show me your home," she said.

He grinned. "We can spend as many days as you want making memories here. But my home is you. It's that little boy we left in Montana, who's probably busy wearing out his auntie Lauren and uncle Tavish. As long as we have each other and we have Ben, we have everything we need."

They did. And knowing she could trust him and trust herself, she knew they always would.

Epilogue

Lauren and Tavish's wedding was beautiful, despite a few weather-related glitches. Zach was relieved to be at the reception—he'd missed squiring Cadie to yesterday's rehearsal due to a heinous search and rescue operation, one of his first since returning to the crew post-injury. And then this morning, a howling blizzard had shut down the ski lifts, and with them, the mid-station lodge. With every available space booked with New Year's Eve festivities, the dinner and dancing had shifted to the foyer of the base lodge.

He sat at his assigned table—he'd been with the Dawson family, but not with Cadie, who'd sat at the head table—and shook his head at how well the wedding party had jazzed up the spacious stone-and-beam rotunda on extremely short notice. The pale wood paneling of the walls added a classy backdrop, and Lauren's eye for detail, plus elbow grease on the part of her family to string up white lights, brought just the right touch of romance to the high-ceilinged entranceway.

Now that the party was in full swing, everyone was alternating between plucking delights from the towering dessert buffet and dancing the night away in anticipation of celebrating the new year with the happy couple. The only problem with this whole day was that he wasn't the one with a ring on his finger at the end of it.

He did have one in his pocket.

His mom had given him his grandmother's engagement ring after she'd first met Cadie the day after filming in Whistler. She'd taken one look at Zach's face and had claimed to know. And who was he to argue with his mom? He'd been carrying the diamond around since. Whether someone else's wedding was the right place to propose, though, he hadn't decided.

Cadie was on the dance floor, arms in the air and singing along to vintage Bon Jovi with Lauren and Garnet. Lauren was still looking pretty spry, despite being seven months pregnant. And Cadie, well...

He tugged at his tie—could probably lose the silk noose at this point—and grimaced. The dark purple gown she wore was high in the front and essentially backless and he wasn't sure what he wanted more—for her to be the one with a round belly or to strip that dress off her and carry her to bed. Which, since they hadn't moved in together yet, they didn't technically share... Another thing to add to the to-do list. It was time.

He took a swig from his beer bottle but the malty flavor didn't appeal as much as the chance to kiss the woman he loved on the dance floor. He set his beer down and crossed the room. Stepping in behind her, he cupped the flare of her hips.

"I'm not sure if I should send a thank-you note or a complaint to whomever picked out this dress," he grumbled, leaning in close to her ear.

"Don't get all caveman on me now, Cardenas." She reached back with her free hand to poke him in the gut.

"Caveman? That's not what I meant. You look stunning, and I'm all over you showing that off. But it's been torture. Do you know how easy it would be for me to slide my hand up the front of this thing?" He palmed her back and teased the edge of the silky fabric where it swooped low along her spine. "I've been having fantasies about you all night."

"Mmm, tell me more." She turned to face him, looping her arms around his neck and downright leveling him with a sultry pout. "Ben's settled. The babysitter's fine. We've got a few more hours to play. No need to stay until midnight. We could take off, go to your place..."

They might still have separate residences, but they'd merged their lives in every other way. After returning from Whistler, Cadie had taken some huge steps to let go of her guilt. The more she processed her feelings, the more they were able to strengthen their relationship. To find joy in the simple things like taking Ben to Saturday art classes or sneaking away for the odd adult-only ski afternoon. To put Ben to bed and then staying up late pleasuring each other beyond expectation, to rely on love to get through the low days.

He intended to rely on that love for the rest of his life. And he didn't want to wait any longer. He wanted to head into the new year with a ring on her finger.

Surely she'd understand his impatience, so long as he didn't make a public spectacle out of the proposal. "Let's go get a bit of fresh air now that the snow's died down." He shucked out of his suit jacket. Draping it over her shoulders, he guided her toward the door that led to the lodge's front veranda. As they passed the stories-high stone fireplace, Cadie's dad caught Zach's eye. Edward gave him a meaningful nod. Okay then. Was he as omniscient as Zach's mom had been? Ah, well, either way, they had support rallied around them. And as long as

Cadie didn't think it was too soon, they could officially start calling themselves a family of three.

He held the door open and she glided through, taller than normal on high heels. It was a mark of having grown up on the mountain that she didn't shiver once they hit the cold air. She walked over to the railing and leaned her forearms on the edge. A small skiff of snow fell from the sky, spritzing his cheeks as he snuggled in behind her. Goose bumps rose on his arms. Yikes, shirtsleeves were not warm enough, even though the temperature wasn't that far below the freezing mark tonight.

"It's beautiful out here," she breathed. "Quite a change from the morning."

"Can't compare to you."

She groaned. "So corny, Zacharias."

"Worth it." He smiled against her ear and stared out at the black silhouettes of trees and the bright white stripe of lights on the snowy groomer running parallel to the quad chair. Snowcats rumbled on nearby runs, making fresh corduroy for the morning.

"You know what you were saying on Christmas Eve, about me adopting Ben?"

She snuggled closer. "Mm-hmm."

"That's what you want?"

"One hundred percent." She paused, tone growing wary. "Is it not what *you* want?"

"I will never change my mind on being a father to Ben." Clearing his now-thick throat, he said, "Want to have a new-year adventure tomorrow? Maybe take Ben in the backpack and snowshoe around the lake?"

"Or we could head out to Aunt Georgie's ranch for a sleigh ride." Nuzzling her cheek against his throat, she swayed to the slow beat of the music carrying from inside the lodge. Her long hair was captured in a complicated hairstyle at the back of her head. A few stray curls tickled his chin.

His heart thumped in an erratic rhythm. He fumbled one-handed in his pants pocket to get the ring out of the box. Pinching it firmly between his fingers, he put his arms back around her, kissed her temple and whispered, "Either way, do you want to do it as my fiancée?"

She stilled in his arms. "What?"

He held up the ring in her line of sight. "Will you end the year right with me, Cadence? Marry me? Please?"

She turned in his arms and clutched his shirtfront. Her wide eyes caught the light from behind him. "Zach…"

With one hand on her back, he held the ring in front of her with the other. "I'd get down on one knee, but the deck's snow grating is a bitch—"

"You're not supposed to propose at someone else's wedding!" she chided.

Ten…nine… The chorus of voices from inside was muted but clear.

"Quick, the countdown." For some reason it mattered to get the diamond on her finger before the clock rolled over. "We won't tell anyone until tomorrow. I love you. Say yes. Please."

A wide grin split her lips and she held up her hand. "Yes! Yes, yes, yes."

Two…one…

He slid the ring on her finger. "Happy New Year."

She admired the sparkling gemstone for a moment before leaning up for a soft kiss. "Happy new life."

* * * * *

Don't miss Lauren and Tavish's story,
From Exes To Expecting,
available now from Harlequin Special Edition!

Available July 16, 2019

#2707 RUST CREEK FALLS CINDERELLA
Montana Mavericks: Six Brides for Six Brothers
by Melissa Senate
When Lily Hunt, a plain-Jane Cinderella chef, gives herself a makeover to spice up her flirtation with a sexy cowboy, she finds herself contending with his past heartbreak and his father's matchmaking scheme!

#2708 ONE NIGHT WITH THE COWBOY
Match Made in Haven • by Brenda Harlen
Soon-to-be-exes Brielle Channing and Caleb Gilmore said goodbye after a night of passion—until a surprise pregnancy changed all their plans. Could their baby be their second chance for happily-ever-after, or will their feuding families once again come between them?

#2709 THEIR INHERITED TRIPLETS
Texas Legends: The McCabes • by Cathy Gillen Thacker
To give the orphaned triplets the stability they need, guardians Lulu McCabe and Sam Kirkland decide to jointly adopt them. But when it's discovered their marriage wasn't actually annulled, they have to prove to the courts they're responsible—by renewing their vows!

#2710 HIS UNEXPECTED TWINS
Small-Town Sweethearts • by Carrie Nichols
It was supposed to be a summer romance between friends, but a surprise pregnancy forces Liam McBride and Ellie Harding to confront their feelings for each other—and their fears of the future.

#2711 THEIR LAST SECOND CHANCE
The Stone Gap Inn • by Shirley Jump
When Melanie Cooper runs into her first love, her picture-perfect life is unraveling—unbeknownst to her family. Harris McCarthy is hiding a few secrets of his own, but exposing them could save Melanie's career and torpedo their last second chance at love.

#2712 A BABY BETWEEN FRIENDS
Sweet Briar Sweethearts • by Kathy Douglass
After their friendship is ruined by a night of passion, Joni Danielson and Lex Devlin have to find a way back to being friends. Will her unexpected pregnancy lead them to love?

Get 4 FREE REWARDS!

We'll send you 2 FREE Books plus 2 FREE Mystery Gifts.

YES! Please send me 2 FREE Harlequin® Special Edition novels and my 2 FREE gifts (gifts are worth about $10 retail). After receiving them, if I don't wish to receive any more books, I can return the shipping statement marked "cancel." If I don't cancel, I will receive 6 brand-new novels every month and be billed just $4.99 per book in the U.S. or $5.74 per book in Canada. That's a savings of at least 12% off the cover price! It's quite a bargain! Shipping and handling is just 50¢ per book in the U.S. and 75¢ per book in Canada.* I understand that accepting the 2 free books and gifts places me under no obligation to buy anything. I can always return a shipment and cancel at any time. The free books and gifts are mine to keep no matter what I decide.

235/335 HDN GMY2

Name (please print)

Address   Apt. #

City   State/Province   Zip/Postal Code

Mail to the Reader Service:
IN U.S.A.: P.O. Box 1341, Buffalo, NY 14240-8531
IN CANADA: P.O. Box 603, Fort Erie, Ontario L2A 5X3

Want to try 2 free books from another series! Call 1-800-873-8635 or visit www.ReaderService.com.

"The two of you are still married," Liz said.

"Still?" Lulu croaked.

Sam asked, "What are you talking about?"

"More to the point, how do you know this?" Lulu
demanded, the news continuing to hit her like a gut punch.

Travis looked down at the papers in front of him.
"Official state records show you eloped in the Double
Knot Wedding Chapel in Memphis, Tennessee, on
Monday, March 14, nearly ten years ago. Alongside
another couple, Peter and Theresa Thompson, in a double
wedding ceremony."

Lulu gulped. "But our union was never legal," she
pointed out, trying to stay calm, while Sam sat beside her
in stoic silence.

Liz countered, "Ah, actually, it is legal. In fact, it's still
valid to this day."

Sam reached over and took her hand in his, much as he had the first time they had been in this room together. "How is that possible?" Lulu asked weakly.

"We never mailed in the certificate of marriage, along with the license, to the state of Tennessee," Sam said.

"And for our union to be recorded and therefore legal, we had to have done that," Lulu reiterated.

"Well, apparently, the owners of the Double Knot Wedding Chapel did, and your marriage was recorded. And is still valid to this day, near as we can tell. Unless you two got a divorce or an annulment somewhere else? Say another country?" Travis prodded.

"Why would we do that? We didn't know we were married," Sam returned.

Don't miss
Their Inherited Triplets *by Cathy Gillen Thacker,*
available August 2019 wherever
Harlequin® Special Edition books and ebooks are sold.

www.Harlequin.com

"I'd have thought the idea of me getting caught in a rainstorm would make your day."

He gave her a quick glance. Just because she was off-limits didn't mean he was blind.

"Trust me, it did." Luke slowed the truck and reached behind the seat to grab his zippered hoodie hanging there. Whitney looked down and her cheeks flamed when she realized how her clothes were clinging to her. She snatched the hoodie from his hand before he could give it to her, and thrust her arms into it without offering any thanks. Even the zipper sounded pissed off when she yanked it closed.

"Perfect. Another guy with more testosterone than manners. Nice to know it's not just a Chicago thing. Jackasses are everywhere."

Luke frowned. He'd been having fun at her expense, figuring she'd give it right back to him as she had before. But her words hinted at a story that didn't reflect well on men in general. She'd been hurt. He shouldn't care. But that quick dimming of the fight in her eyes made him feel ashamed. *That* was a new experience.

A flash of lightning made her flinch. But the thunder didn't follow as quickly as the last time. The storm was moving off. He drove from the vineyard into the parking lot and over to the main house. The sound of the rain on the roof was less angry. But Whitney wasn't. She was clutching his sweatshirt around herself, her knuckles white. From anger? Embarrassment? Both? Luke shook his head.

"Look, I thought I was doing the right thing, driving up there." He rubbed the back of his neck and grimaced, remembering how sweaty and filthy he still was. "It's not my fault you walked out of the woods soaking wet. I mean, I try not to be a jackass, but I'm still a man. And I *did* offer my hoodie."

Whitney's chin pointed up toward the second floor of the main house. Her neck was long and graceful. There was a vein pulsing at the base of it. She blinked a few times, and for a horrifying moment, he thought there might be tears shimmering there in her eyes. *Damn it.* The last thing he needed was to have Helen's niece *crying* in his truck. He opened his mouth to say something—anything—but she beat him to it.

"I'll concede I wasn't prepared for rain." Her mouth barely moved, her words forced through clenched teeth. "But a gentleman would have looked away or…something."

His low laughter was enough to crack that brittle shell of hers. She turned to face him, eyes wide.

"See, Whitney, that's where you made your biggest mistake." He shrugged. "It wasn't going out for a day hike with a storm coming." He talked over her attempted objection. "Your *biggest* mistake was thinking I'm any kind of gentleman."

The corner of her mouth tipped up into an almost smile. "But you said you weren't a jackass."

"There's a hell of a lot of real estate between jackass and gentleman, babe."

Her half smile faltered, then returned. That familiar spark appeared in her eyes. The crack in her veneer had been repaired, and the sharp edge returned to her voice. Any other guy might have been annoyed, but Luke was oddly relieved to see Whitney back in fighting form.

"The fact that you just referred to me as 'babe' tells me you're a lot closer to jackass than you think."

He lifted his shoulder. "I never told you which end of the spectrum I fell on."

The rain had slowed to a steady drizzle. She reached for the door handle, looking over her shoulder with a smirk.

"Actually, I'm pretty sure you just did."

She hurried up the steps to the covered porch. He waited, but she didn't look back before going into the house. Her energy still filled the cab of the truck, and so did her scent. Spicy, woodsy, rain soaked. Finally coming to his senses, he threw the truck into Reverse and headed back toward the carriage house. He needed a long shower. A long *cold* one.

Don't miss
Jo McNally's Slow Dancing at Sunrise,
available July 2019 from HQN Books!

www.Harlequin.com

PHJMEXP0719